"INNOVATOR RON JONES HAS MADE A CAREER OF GRAPPLING WITH CHALLENGES OTHERS SHIRK.

"'I'm blessed,' says Ron Jones. 'I'm smitten by the angels of innocence I work with, people who grab you by the hand, talk nonsense by the hour, eat with protruding tongues and have bowel movements at the wrong time.' Adds wife Deanna: 'What better job could he have? He gets to play all day.'

"Jones's current playground is San Francisco's widely acclaimed Recreation Center for the Handicapped, where he has been physical education director since 1978. His charges are 1,200 impaired children and adults, and he has had remarkable success with them."

—*People Magazine*

SAY RAY

Ron Jones

with illustrations by
SANDY CLIFFORD

BANTAM BOOKS
TORONTO • NEW YORK • LONDON • SYDNEY • AUCKLAND

SAY RAY

A Bantam Book / July 1984

ISBN 0-553-24349-7

Published simultaneously in the United States and Canada

*Bantam Books are published by Bantam Books, Inc. Its trade-
mark, consisting of the words "Bantam Books" and the por-
trayal of a rooster, is Registered in U.S. Patent and Trademark
Office and in other countries. Marca Registrada. Bantam
Books, Inc., 666 Fifth Avenue, New York, New York 10103.*

PRINTED IN THE UNITED STATES OF AMERICA

O   0 9 8 7 6 5 4 3 2 1

About This Story

Say Ray is in its essentials a true story. The names of the actors, however, have been changed. Events in the story, much of the dialogue, and certain descriptions had to be re-created with the aid of documents secured from the San Francisco Office of Social Services, the San Francisco public guardian's office, and the Office of Tourist Affairs. Uruapan, Mexico. Special thanks to Billie Mills and Richard Heus for help with research.

Say Ray is dedicated to the San Francisco Recreation Center for the Handicapped and to the Special Olympics.

Prologue

Ray Martinez loved the swings in Children's Playground. In fact, one particular swing. It was a strange sight, Ray Martinez being the age he was—a grown man, twenty-three years old. Slouched in the web seat of his favorite swing. Gently moving back and forth. His tennis shoes tapping the ground like toe shoes of a ballet dancer. Back and forth. For hours he would sit in the swing, prancing forward and back.

Each swaying movement was accompanied by the soft groan of chain against metal rings and an even softer humming from Ray. He was always humming the same song. It sounded like Elvis Presley's "Love Me Tender." Or maybe "Happy Birthday." It was hard to tell. His mouth held a perpetual smile. And his eyes were hooded by an always-present baseball cap. A black and orange cap with the San Francisco Giants in script.

Ray Martinez is a man you have probably met, particularly if you live in San Francisco. Maybe you've passed him on the street—that man who seemed a little unkempt. Who didn't look like he belonged to anything. Or was going anyplace in particular. Who walked with his arms wrapped around his body, as if he were holding himself together. Kept getting in people's way. His shirt soiled. Probably drunk. When he smiled at you, you looked away. Was he dangerous? you wondered. Surely unpredictable and useless. Sick, maybe. And stupid.

If you met him on a bus, he was sitting in the front. Always in the front, close to the driver. Holding a transfer as if it were a flag. Smiling. Talking gibberish to everyone who lurches down the aisle. Why doesn't he get his teeth fixed? He could be handsome. In a way, he looks like some movie star. Like Marlon Brando, maybe, in that film with Karl Malden as the sheriff. Yes, that's it; he looks like Marlon Brando—kind of a Mexican Marlon Brando. It's those talking eyes and long sideburns. Funny, he's the only one on the bus who tries to be friendly.

You can also find Ray walking down Market Street on San Francisco's theater row, facing the life-size billboard of Sean Connery or ogling the naked promises of a skin flick. Or you can find him on the park bench across from the Washington Street Bar and Grill, sitting with his head propped in both hands, murmuring some ancient prayer. And he is the man on the swing in Golden Gate Park's Children's Playground.

Of all "Ray's places" in San Francisco, the swing in the park is his favorite. "His" swing is the one closest to the merry-go-round, and it faces the cement fountain. From "his" swing, Ray can listen to the wheezing calliope of the merry-go-round and watch the children play in the sand.

Ray enjoys children. Mostly because they talk to him when their parents aren't looking. And they like it when Ray brings a handful of water from the drinking faucet so they can make sand cookies and doughnuts. If the parents that circle the sandbox would let him, Ray would gladly bring the children all the handfuls of water they wanted. But of course parents don't like this bedraggled man who leaves his pants open while playing with their children. They worry out loud that he's a pervert or a child molester. After all, no other adults try to talk with their children. He must be crazy—bringing them water in his hands. They warn Ray to *stay away*, or they'll tell the police.

So Ray sits in his swing and enjoys the gentle movement and the sight of his friends playing in the sand. No one yells at him when he sits on the swing. And he keeps his secret. It started months ago. In the morning, he places paper cups filled with water on the ledge of the sandbox. The children are the only ones who know it's a gift from the man on the swing. And the only ones who notice that the man on the swing is smiling.

Swinging in the same place, the same way, for hours at a time allowed Ray to vanish. I mean you simply forgot he was there. He became a part of the scenery. Like the cement benches, the pond, the slide—Ray was uneventful. And eventually unnoticed. In a way, it was a form of human camouflage. This blending in. Never speaking out. Always following the same routine. Sitting in the swing. Like a human timepiece. Moving forward and back. Almost invisible.

For Ray, and for most of us, life is as regular and predictable as swinging in a park. Oh, there might be rough spots and struggles. And sometimes we seem to evolve and change. But for the most part we live in an orderly place without Cinderella miracles, divine interventions, or magnificent adventures. We simply disappear.

When a person has the courage to struggle out of this normal order and begins to make a radical change in his life—when he refuses to vanish—he deserves attention. And sometimes admiration. The story you are about to read is a true story about a number of amazing changes in the life of the man on the swing. These changes began when Ray Martinez suddenly inherited twenty-five thousand dollars.

Ray Martinez, a man called "incompetent" by social-welfare criteria and "unworthy of communion" by his church, could not write his address, read a road sign, or give change for a dollar bill. His father was dead, and his stepmother discarded him into the welfare system, hoping to keep his inheritance for herself while at the same time getting rid of "her problem." All she needed was a simple signature. Ray's signature.

In the welfare system, Ray was classified as abandoned and indigent—without a family willing to care for him and unable to make a living on his own. He was granted welfare status and placed in the board-and-care facility of Mrs. Burr. Mrs. Burr was famous for taking the welfare checks of her "live-ins" and spending the money on dog food for her "chee-chee" dogs and chocolates for herself. In the welfare department, she was known as the Octopus Lady. The nickname came from the way she squinted, the jaundice yellow in her eyes, and the flabs of fat that jiggled around her chin and arms every time she spoke.

Mrs. Burr's passion for chocolates was notorious. The joke among welfare workers was that she fed her chee-chees chocolate while her clients got Alpo— "Those that were lucky, that is!" No one ever wanted to shake her hand or have her fill out a form, because her fingers were always greasy with chocolate. She would squeak in a pinched voice about "taking care of her people," but her fingers told you what her real and only interest was.

The trouble was that the welfare people needed her. She took the sickly and dangerous clients that no one else wanted. And there had been lots of candidates since the closing of the state mental hospitals. She had her long-range plans, a chain of board-and-care homes and a big house for herself. And she might consider letting her worthless stepson, that John Henry Butler, sort of run things—her way. There was lots of money to be made in board and care. She received the monthly welfare check for each client she took in. She could spend the money any way she saw fit as long as those in her charge got two meals and a place to sleep. And there was the side money: Old people and crazy people always got furniture, radios, old clothes—stuff that Butler and she could sell—on the side. And sometimes these clients had money stashed or relatives that sent money and gifts in the mail. And sometimes, as in the case of Ray Martinez, a relative or a lawyer tried to get one of her clients to "sign papers." No one signs any papers in Mrs. Burr's house without her first "looking into it."

John Henry Butler looked just the opposite of his stepmother. He was about the same age as Ray, blond and slender as a switchblade. He hadn't been too successful in school. Or in anything, for that matter. But that never stopped him from rattling off a flood of scams, accomplishments, and plans.

And now, the sudden prospect of Ray Martinez's inheritance changed everything. It was the chance of a lifetime! Mrs. Burr wasn't in good enough health to become Ray's legal guardian, so the job was going to be his! That was the scheme. Mrs. Burr got a lawyer to do the legal work. It was easy.

All Butler had to do was say a few "I dos" in front of a judge. There would be no checks into his record or questions. Just a few promises. Then Butler was supposed to turn over the inheritance money to Mrs. Burr and the lawyer. That was the way it was supposed to work. But he had his own ideas. Plans of his own.

He hated being stuck in the Burr house doing all the dirty work. Getting paid a lousy fifty bucks a week. All his life he felt he was doing time for someone else, taking the chances for someone else. He hated the dogs and that old woman sitting in the corner of her plastic-covered couch. Never letting him sit down or even have a piece of chocolate. Hated her bragging. She wasn't as smart as she thought. Not this time. Now he was finally going to go for the ride. Besides, he and Ray, they were friends. And there was all that money!

For Miss Sherry Croce, Ray's social worker, his new money meant more paper work. More problems. Everything seemed to be going wrong. Sherry Croce had made a career out of social service. She had worked in the same office at the same job for the past seventeen years. Her coworkers and clients had become her only family. With the simultaneous closing of the state hospitals and the federal government takeover of welfare payments, well, she didn't know what to do. Her case load jumped from manageable to impossible. At the same time, the former function of the local office—issuing checks and assisting clients—was being taken over by the Feds. People she knew and cared for, people she felt responsible for, were abruptly told to apply to federal assistance. Inexplicably, they were without benefits and trapped in a paper war to prove their eligibility for the new programs.

She had never felt so helpless. So lost.

And now, on top of this, came Ray Martinez. She couldn't find out from anybody how much money Ray was to inherit. Or what would happen to his welfare status once the money was gone. And most important, she began to worry about Ray's safety. She had a feeling that something was terribly wrong.

In desperation, she asked a coworker for help. J. B. Carver and Sherry Croce had been sharing lunch dates for six years. It was their regular, informal, don't forget get-together. So it was not unusual for them to discuss a case. Particularly a case involving money. After all, money was a big part of J. B. Carver's job. Carver was the department's investigator in charge of fraud and criminal activity—one of the jobs about to be phased out. When J. B. Carver agreed to look into Ray's case, he knew it would be his last assignment, and he wanted to do it right—for himself and for his friend, Miss Sherry Croce.

As for Ray Martinez, the inheritance meant that he

got a new electric guitar from Mrs. Burr. Something he'd always wanted. Just like Elvis. It wasn't really new; the electric cord was missing, but that really didn't matter. And he got his own room. Best of all, he got to keep his radio instead of giving it to Mrs. Burr as she said was going to happen. And John Henry Butler and he were becoming friends.

Initial Service

February 13, 1970

    Mr. Raymond Martinez, male, age twenty-three, applied for ATD (Aid to Totally Disabled) 1/19/70. Certified for aid as an incompetent person 2/13/70.

Reason for Referral

    Mr. Martinez has been living with his employed stepmother and is an orphan. Date of parent's death is unknown. His stepmother, who is employed in a beauty shop, is moving Sunday, February 15, 1970. She has refused to take him with her and wants him to be placed in a boarding home. She feels she has no responsibility for him.

Evaluation of Functioning

    Mr. Martinez is a man of medium build and height. He is mentally retarded (WAIS IQ VERBAL 56 PERFORMANCE 66). He cannot be expected to find his way around town or manage money or any of his affairs. He is better able to handle concrete, nonverbal tasks than verbal and abstract tasks. He tries, but even on tasks he can do, he fears failure and needs support. The psychological examination indicates the client was very upset that "he might not have any place to go" and fears being "put away." Apparently, the stepmother no longer wishes him to reside with her.

Services Provided

    A boarding home has been found for Mr. Martinez at 970 Fulton Street. Mrs. Burr is the operator and will pick up Mr. Martinez; ATD payments of $230 per month will be issued for board and care. Plan home visits to get to know Mr. Martinez and to complete an evaluation of the home in terms of care and suitability.

Croce 2/13/70

Sherry Croce closed the file. Everything was in order. The Initial Information Report (DA-I) attached to certification (DA-3), the medical examination, and finally her disposition of the case. She was pleased at the order of things and the service it promised. A "person in need" had come into the San Francisco Office of Social Service, and within thirty days that "client" had been evaluated and granted the appropriate service. Miss Croce almost smiled as she placed the case file in her Foremost box. Thank goodness for Foremost milk cartons. Those convenient boxes used by Foremost to deliver milk to local stores. They were sturdy cardboard boxes with handles on each side. Just perfect for storing file folders. Everyone in the social service division had their supply of milk boxes. The social-service dispositions of the needs of the city's alcoholics, mentally troubled, blind, and disabled sat in these cardboard caves.

Miss Croce liked order. Maybe that's why she entered social work. Putting disarrayed lives into something close to normal living. And there was also this sense of fraternity working in the department of social services. I mean, she knew everyone from secretaries to fraud investigators to supervisors. Everyone in the department had studied for the civil service exams at Mabel Boxes' on Balboa and Eighth Avenue. Everyone had learned to prepare their reports in the same way. And most everyone in the department was proud of their work. In a way, it was their department. Their family.

The San Francisco Department of Social Services handled everything from screening prospective clients to providing income and care. One unique practice of the department created by Miss Croce and other "line workers" was the substitute payee plan. If a client needed help managing their finances, a worker would help them set up a checking account and, if that didn't work, would pay local merchants to keep the clients in food, cigarettes, toilet items, and clothing. It was this personalized work that Miss Croce and others took pride in. But according to the flow charts surrounding those interdepartmental meetings, it was that personalized aid that was in jeopardy.

What was going to happen to all this once the Feds took over? There was so many rumors. Even the possibility that local welfare offices would close. Hallway conversation, stairwell gossip, had it that the Feds were planning to take over determining who would be eligible for aid and then issue payments directly to those who qualify for assistance. Actually send welfare checks in the mail, from some center in Alabama. And replace local interviews and screening in favor of mailed questionnaires. Sherry Croce was angry at this insensitive "takeover." How are her clients who can't read or write going to fill out paper work evaluating their financial status? And send "evidence of income" to some place in Washington, D.C.? Since the Federal Income Form for Compliance asked recipients of aid to show how much money they had, most of her clients would simply wad up the change in their pockets and mail it off to Washington. And if they did qualify for aid, well, a check would come in the mail, and they would immediately spend or lose it. Or it would be stolen. There was no personal service, no plan to help the disabled make decisions about their money. No means to see if care was being received. For Sherry and her coworkers, the federal promise of more aid for the disabled was actually a disaster waiting to happen. Or, as Jim Carver called it, "one way to cut the welfare rolls and put a lot of people like you and me—out of a job!"

Sherry Croce was a woman who waited. She had been waiting for as long as she could remember. Growing up in the Sunset District of San Francisco, she lived on a block where every house looked like the one next door. Every person looked like the person next door. Row after row, avenue after avenue, these white stucco houses stood like dominoes waiting for the next earthquake. And the people who lived inside them were also always standing and waiting. Waiting for their children to grow up and graduate. Waiting for the right spouse, the right job, the final blessing. In the Sunset District, there were no exceptions. Sherry Croce was no exception.

For Sherry, nothing was ever lost or out of place. She did everything that was asked of her by parents, teachers, and employers. She always brushed her teeth, wore pleated skirts and high-buttoned blouses from I. Magnins, carefully combed her red hair into a tight bun, smelled of Palmolive hand cream, and applied just the right amount of Maybelline eye liner and lip shine. She was wearing the same clothes at age thirty-eight that she had worn at eighteen. She took pride in the way she looked and the job she held. Found it hard to understand the hippies with their Salvation Army appearance and their "do it now" philosophy.

Like everyone she grew up with, it was proper to be waiting for something to happen. I guess that's why Sherry was attracted to J. B. Carver. He was just the opposite. He was always running around lost, always losing things. He was always stepping on someone's toes in the welfare department, always getting in trouble with the district attorney's office. She couldn't understand someone who acted impulsively and who wasn't waiting to get married.

Carver grew up in East Oakland in what was then called a "colored" neighborhood. The houses were big and sunny, with lots of people coming and going. As a child, James Carver was the first kid on his street to ride his bike to San Francisco. He smuggled his bike on the old A Train by putting it in a sack and telling the conductor it was a base fiddle with wheels. Once in San Francisco, he got so excited and visited so many places that he forgot where he'd left his bike. It had been thirty years since he rode his bike as a six-year-old through the streets of "the City." But still he quipped, "That bike of mine is still out there, and one of these days I'm going to find it."

Carver enjoyed being a detective. "For a person who always loses things, it's only natural to join a profession that finds things." Of course, in his own mind, his own things would always "show up" or be where he could put his hands on them. This was wildly untrue.

Sherry went to see her friend Carver in his office. She studied him as he swung around in his swivel chair. His elbow struck a pile of papers, sending them fluttering toward the floor. He smiled. It was a contagious smile. Carver was round like a beach ball. Everything about him was round. The cheeks in his face, the open eyes, the radar-dome hair, the instant and wonderful smile. Even the way he sat in his chair. He didn't just sit in a chair; he overwhelmed it.

Sherry laughed. "So where's your tie? We're supposed to be going to lunch, remember?"

In a dramatic flurry, Carver opened his desk drawer, and like a magician, pulled out a silk tie. "And ladies and gentlemen, what do you call this!"

"Yes," Sherry applauded, "and that gives you two, the one in your hand and the one falling out of your pants pocket."

Carver swiveled away, searching for his jacket.

"It's hanging there, on the door."

As the two walked down the corridor, their shoes clicked against the waxed linoleum, reverberating louder each time they passed an office partition.

Carver was doing most of the talking. "Finding someone isn't a matter of knowing where to look; it's knowing the person you're looking for—" As Carver spoke, he realized Sherry had turned sullen and was retreating into some distant thought. This had been happening a lot lately, and he didn't like it. "You know what's bothering you—really got you worried the most—isn't this Ray fellow or your other clients, it's this transition—you're afraid of losing your job!"

Sherry didn't answer, but she did quicken her walk. She could see her office at the end of the hall and the stairwell leading to the street.

"I tell you what it is," Carver repeated. "You're not going to like it, but it's your job—you, me, and everyone else around here, we're all afraid of losing our jobs, it's got nothing to do with the welfare of our case loads!"

Sherry snapped back almost in a sob. "You, always being the detective."

"Yeah, but I'm right."

"Partly, partly."

"Sherry, you know, you and I been dealing with this for quite a while—feelings we can't act on."

Sherry grabbed the doorknob to her office. She stared into Carver's eyes as he continued to talk.

"Feeling afraid of losing your job and not being able to take care of yourself is all right."

Sherry forcibly twisted the door handle and let the frosted glass door swing open.

"Taking care of yourself," Carver was still explaining, "you're going to have to—you can't do every case, do everything like you used to—let go, it's going to be hard, there's more to life than—"

Sherry Croce pulled free of Carver and took one step into her office.

Carver didn't follow.

Sherry was shaking, but her voice was calm, almost deliberate. "You don't know anything about feelings or about me, anything." She closed the door with a bang against the metal frame.

Carver stood for a moment. He could see the impression of Sherry's back pushed up against the frosted glass of the door. Wiping his eyes and face with one hand, he softly uttered, "Shit."

Sherry Croce waited for what seemed a long time. She stood looking at her desk and carefully positioned office plants. Studied the crude portrait drawing that hung next to the file cabinet. It was a gift from one of her clients. No one could figure out what the lines and colors were meant to depict. She walked to her file cabinet and traced its metallic face with two fingers. Her file cabinet was her one rebellion in life. Against all departmental and government regulations, she had painted it baby blue.

Miss Croce reexamined the list of clients on her desk top. On the top of the list of people to see, she printed in the name Ray Martinez.

Ray Martinez was her latest case. With this assignment, she reached her active case-load limit of 60 cases. She wouldn't have any more interruptions for a while. She could get out of the office, get away from interdepartmental meetings, and get into the street. That's where the real work is. Subconsciously crossing one arm in front of her body, she reached for her shoulder and began to massage the tightness. Her shoulder and back had been bothering her.

Seeing the new name on her list, she wondered what this Raymond Martinez would be like. They were all so different and wonderful, her clients. Each had some frailty but also some hidden interest and capacity. It never failed to amaze her. There was "Preacher," who could eat a steak with his gums. And "Sweet Philip" in his green suit and bow tie. "Kirkwood," the man who never went outdoors. Each case was a challenge, probably similar to raising children. Getting them to be as independent as possible, as free and as strong as life would allow. Yes—Sherry inwardly smiled and tapped the list.

She would have to see if she could get Raymond in a recreation program at the Recreation Center for the Handicapped. Maybe get him involved in the Special Olympics. Make sure Mrs. Burr's board-and-care operation is up to code. She pondered with anticipation the prospect of her latest client's liking flowers, opera, maybe bowling, or maybe he might enjoy visiting the park. Next to the name Ray Martinez, Sherry scrawled the notation "Chinese food," then silently congratulated herself. I bet he likes Chinese food.

September 7, 1971

Quarterly Evaluation
Martinez, Raymond
#03-016-9657

Housing Suitability

After repeated efforts to force Mrs. Burr into improving the living arrangements for Ray, things are suddenly better. Ray has his own room, and the bedding is washed. The dogs (I counted twenty-three on one visit) are now limited to the backyard. Mrs. Burr indicates that things are improving for her. She has been talking with the redevelopment agency, and they have promised her a reconstructed building on Steiner Street. In fact, Mrs. Burr mentioned operating several homes by the end of the year if she could get her son John Henry to learn "the business."

There are two new clients in the Burr house. A couple named Rogers, Larry and Jocelyn Rogers. They are elderly and somewhat senile, but they might be better company for Ray than the previous tenants placed in the Burr house as part of a drug rehabilitation program. Mr. Rogers seems to like baseball and has his own radio—again, something new for residents of the Burr house.

Mrs. Burr reports that Ray's use of lighters and smelting tin cans is a dangerous hobby and potential fire hazard. However, she has now allowed him to do this at appropriate times so she can watch him. She says she likes Ray and that he's quite helpful around the house. Mrs. Burr asked about the procedures for becoming Ray's legal guardian, because she'd like to assure him that he has a permanent place. She has Ray calling her "Mom."

Inheritance Issue
Summary of Contacts

Both Mrs. Burr and Ray told me about a possible inheritance from the estate of Ray's father. Ray spoke excitedly about "being rich," that he "owned a lot of houses," and Mrs. Burr "let me go out and buy an electric guitar. I got to buy, go out and get this guitar." Ray carries his guitar around with him. It's bright purple with reflector buttons that spell out WHIZ. I don't know where Ray got the guitar, but he bought it without the electrical cord or amplifier. Perhaps it is a leftover from one of the previous tenants. In the middle of conversation with Ray, he will stand up and posture like some rock star on the Ed Sullivan Show. Ray says, he's "rich now and going to be a rock music man, like on television and buy Mrs. Burr a new Cadillac or any color car I want ..." Ray also offers to buy me a new Cadillac.

Evidently, the stepmother asked Ray to sign some papers, but Mrs. Burr suggested he wait and talk with his worker. I've telephoned the stepmother several times about this. She has recently remarried and wants to sell the house inherited by her and Raymond upon the death of Ray's father on Thanksgiving Day 1965. I informed the stepmother that if Ray were entitled to any estate, her attorney should set up a trust fund for Raymond. The stepmother says there has been no real income from the property over the past six years and that taxes, depreciation, and upkeep have resulted in money out of her pocket and now she wants to sell the property to recoup that loss. The stepmother's attorney, Mr. Juris Kopecki (545-6060), called me to inquire about the legal status of Raymond, specifically, who acts as the legal guardian. Mrs. Burr and I attended a meeting with Mr. Bell of the San Francisco Neighborhood Legal Assistance. They refused to handle the case because it involved property. In a similar decision, the attorney for the Legal Aid Society decided that there was too much money involved for their participation.

Mrs. Burr has solicited the aid of an attorney, Mr. Jonathan R. Wilkins (877-8311), to give Ray advice on his rights and receivership of his share of the estate. On 8/26/71, Mr. Wilkins arranged (without notification to this office) for a legal guardian to help Ray administer his affairs. The legal guardian is Mr. John Henry Butler, the stepson of Mrs. Burr.

Plan of Action

I plan to check on the father's will. If the will

was probated, there should be some record. I am very concerned about this guardianship arrangement. The attorneys in this matter seem uncooperative and very evasive about the possible sale of estate property and the manner in which Ray will be protected, so I plan to keep in close touch with individuals involved in this case.

Croce 9/7/71

Addendum

9/20/71, Mr. Kopecki called and said that he would be sending a check for $1,280.87 to Raymond to cover the amount of net rent that was due Raymond. Mr. Kopecki has been informed that Raymond now has a guardian and legal help and that this amount can be verified only after everyone involved has seen the expenses in arriving at the net rent figure.

Croce 9/20/71

Ice Cream Shouldn't
Be Allowed To Melt

<u>December 12, 1971</u>

Mrs. Burr and her son were arguing. Their voices crashed about the house. Ray closed his door and turned on his radio. He expected the Giants but instead got the Chipmunks singing, "Santa Claus Is Coming to Town." Ray did his version of a sing-along.

> *You better watch out*
> *You better not doubt*
> *You better be good, nice and good*
> *Santa Claus is coming to,*
> *Come to town.*

Before Ray could finish his sing-along, John Henry Butler was standing in the doorway.

"Say, Ray, you ever had a Christmas, I mean a real Christmas, presents all over the place and a stocking you know full of things, candy, batteries for your radio, and chewing gum?"

Butler answered his own question. "I never had one myself, not in this house, and now you know what she wants and she gets it usually that is . . ."

Ray was listening as hard as he could, but the words were coming so fast. So he shrugged his shoulders and answered, "Yes."

Butler kept on speaking like a speeding car going past a stop sign. "She wants me to give her our money to buy a house over on Valencia. And you know what we get out of the deal? Our own room and television. Didn't ask me or nothin'! Just goes ahead and plans to buy this house thinkin' she's some kind of real estate genius. Ray turn down that radio it's drivin' me nutty. I don't know who she—"

Ray turned off his radio and carefully tucked it under the bed pillow. Undaunted by John Henry's pacing, Ray began to mumble,

> *You better be nice,*
> *Nice and good*
> *You better be good*
> *'Cause Santa Claus*
> *Is coming to town*
> *He sees you went to sleeping . . .*

"That's right," Butler persisted. "Once, once in my life, I get this Christmas present, right in my lap, takin' care of you, being this guardian and you know tryin' to do it right, maybe get us some Christmas presents. But oh no, she's got these plans. Always got these big plans. When do I get plans? That's what I want to know. She goes out and buys this sofa and hi-fidelity stereo for the new house, she says . . ."

> *So you better be good*
> *You better be right*
> *Santa . . .*

"Ray, is that radio still on? I thought I told you to turn that thing off!" Butler pushed his hands through his blond hair. "Are you listening to me, man? I'm trying to save your life!"

Ray acknowledged the frown in Butler's face. He stopped humming and tried to make conversation. "I turned on the radio, no Giants tonight—Willie Mays hit the six hundred and forty-sixth home run against Cincinnati—bye-bye, baby." Ray was smiling. Hoping he had said the right thing.

"Hold it, wait a second, don't want to get started on that baseball stuff. I'm talkin' about us getting out of here, you understand, takin' charge of things, splittin', making our own plans."

Ray looked up. Understood the anxious tone in Butler's voice. "The radio, I turned the radio, it's off."

Butler wasn't finished. "It's you and me against the lady down there. She'll take us to the cleaners unless we pull some aces of our own—what do you say? You and me together sorta breakin' out of this place?"

Ray was enthusiastic. He would do anything. Anything asked of him. "I can do it," he gladly replied.

Satisfied with this pledge, Butler's tongue was winding down. "That woman downstairs, she never gave us no Christmas, never will. She's mean. Oh, I've seen it first hand. . . ."

As John Henry ranted, Ray's attention turned toward the window that faced the street. A methodical rain was tapping on the sill. Streaks of water slowly spread down the pane of glass, tiny rivers constantly vanishing and renewing. Ray traced one of these rivulets with a finger. The fog on the cool lower part of the window gave evidence of the path of his finger as it pointed toward the street below.

Butler slowed his talking, then stopped. Ray and the window and the vision of the rain-polished street transfixed him. The telephone lines and Muni cables swayed. Drops gathered on these black threads like acrobats on a circus wire. At first, they clustered tightly in place. Then they raced together and tumbled into darkness. Gathering again on the slickened street, the acrobats glistened with new life. And then, just for a moment, all the lights on the street were bouncing free of their prisons—fragmenting and dancing in wetness. Automobile lamps chased the falling water, giving it the sight of silver tinsel. Reflecting ponds of neon light pushed against moving curbs, appearing and vanishing with the passing of each car. You could hear the water squeezing under tires. Falling into deep storm drains. Slapping against the window.

Drawn to the rhythm and sight of this winter rain, both men watched in silence. How much time had passed? A second. An hour. They didn't know. Then both slumped against the wall and stretched their legs. Butler was the first to speak. His voice was now low and quiet, almost conversational. "So, Ray, tell me, what do you want to do with this fortune of yours? Don't just sit there grinning at me for cryin' out loud, come on tell me, you can have anything you want!"

Ray enjoyed the attention. He looked with pleasure at his good friend John Henry Butler. This was the man who came and helped Mrs. Burr take him away from his stepmother's home. Four men came and Mrs. Burr. And he was just finishing dinner when he heard the doorbell. Didn't get dessert. He saw the dessert, some ice cream melting in its container on the table. He didn't know Mrs. Burr or the others, but they grabbed his arm till it hurt. The suitcase was at the door, and Butler carried it out. Didn't let him finish dinner or have the ice cream. Just took him to this room. This house. John Henry Butler didn't eat ice cream. Always gave it to someone. Mrs. Burr didn't like that. She wanted it if there was going to be extra. Ice cream shouldn't be allowed to melt!

Butler asked again. "Say Ray, come on, it's yours, name the ticket and it's yours."

Ray answered, "Ice cream."

"Holy cow, ice cream? I'm offerin' you paradise, some walking clothes, maybe, you know some kinda silk shirt. Don't you want something that turns the girls around?"

"Do you like melted ice cream? I don't like melted ice cream," Ray interrupted. As Ray spoke, he grabbed his guitar and took the stance of a guitar player about to hit a killer chord. In slow motion, Ray stroked the strings of his guitar. The metallic noise didn't match his majestic "Statue of Liberty" pose.

Butler circled the frozen rock star like a slowly dollying camera, stepping in exaggerated giant steps around the still musician—trying to understand this man he was asked to care for. There he stood, a grinning guitar player listening to the applause of some unseen audience. Ray was dressed in the same clothes—those black slacks and pullover shirt—that he was wearing when Butler saw him the night they picked him up. Like then, the zipper on Ray's pants was open. And those huge shoes. The laces were tangled in a glob, with the loose ends tucked into his socks. Ray's clothes smelled soiled and unwashed and full of dried piss.

All this was going to change. Even if Mrs. Burr, damn it, said otherwise. What did she care. It was business with her. Get everything you can. He was going to do it different. This was his chance. And Ray's. He could teach Ray things, get him to take care of himself, tie his shoes and look good. He was handsome, not bad looking if only he had some clothes and would stop playing that game with his guitar, standing there like an idiot.

Finally, Butler stopped his slow-motion survey and spoke. "All I wanted to tell you man is, I just got to get us out of this place, you and me. I'm gonna take care of you, I promise." John Henry's warmth, the relaxed hands at his side, the earnest look in his eyes, all inspired Ray to reach out and try to hug his friend. But since Butler couldn't tell whether Ray was about to hit him over the head with a WHIZ guitar or kiss him, he was backpedaling like mad.

Then, with both hands clenched in front of his face, John Henry put a barrage of words between himself and Ray. "No, don't do that man—put it down—wait, wait, no men don't hug each other, come on, no—that's better!"

"I just wanted to come up here and, you know, wish you a Merry Christmas, you know, ask you what you want. You know, what can I get you for a Christmas present?" John Henry Butler was out the door before the last words were out of his mouth.

Ray walked across the room to his bed. Found his radio under the pillow. And turned it on.

Elvis Presley Has A Ponytail

Ideas—the pictures of how the world works—come to Ray not as a consequence of some questioning, dream, or orderly assembly but as happy mistakes. Unwanted surprises. Missed connections and unexplained pain. One moment people smile at you and want to spend time with you. The next they scowl and close their door. People like your music. Then they hate it. It feels good to take your shoes off. Everyone else seems to like wearing shoes. Orange Muni buses run by your house. Some stop at the corner. Others roar past. There are tiny Christmas lights framing your window, not in other windows. Not in any other window in Mrs. Burr's house. Or any house on the block. They have been there forever, and they don't work.

Unable to explain this world of surprise, Ray finds solace in things that repeat. The radio is Ray's best friend. "KSFO in San Francisco." The same voice every day. The same news. And baseball's "Bye-bye, baby!" That's what Lon Simons—he's the sportscaster—says every time the Giants get a home run, and that's great. Always exciting. Everybody likes baseball. And the *Brady Bunch*. They're on TV. Mr. Brady and Mrs. Brady, and they each have four—or is it three?—children. And they love each other. If Ray could be somebody, he'd probably choose Mrs. Brady, because she's pretty. And she repeats herself. Like Lon Simons of the Giants. Ray can predict what he's going to say and do. He even memorizes some of the things he says. Of course this makes Ray feel good. And of course it confuses the people around him. They talk about the weather or Nixon's troubles while Ray answers with a quotation from the *Brady Bunch* or a Giant statistic.

Because "change" has no meaning for Ray, the radio and TV substitute for the comfort of familiarity. They are always "on." There when you want them. The changing route number on a bus or the changing days of the month or changing how one might travel to work are without meaning for Ray. They have no place in his experience. Ray's world has no history or extension. And his daily routines are the only things that connect these things and make sense out of them. For Ray, *time* is the moment he is in. *Place* is a room and the daily routine tied to that room.

Ray once tried to master part of this confusion by scratching a mark on his arm with a ball-point pen every time he shaved. These were "his days." Soon his arm was filled with marks. He was proud of the calendar. Finally, he couldn't hold in the pleasure of the secret any longer. Had to show it to someone. See their delight in his work. Maybe get a prize like on television.

When he rolled up his sleeve, Mrs. Burr screamed. Thought he was on drugs. Scrubbed the arm till it was raw and bleeding. Satisfied that the railroad of lines were pen tracks, she removed the villain pen from his top drawer. "Never use something like this again," she commanded. "You want to kill yourself? Sticking yourself like that, stupid, just plain stupid! What am I to do with you? Just how am I always supposed to be watching you? You're going to kill yourself one of these days or drive me to an early grave—scaring me like that!"

The top drawer of Ray's dresser contained Ray's most personal treasures. So Mrs. Burr shouldn't have taken the pen. It was his. Besides, the pen didn't do anything bad. After she'd gone back downstairs to her television, Ray opened and angrily closed the drawer. Listening for the roll of the pen and the thump of his radio. The rolling noise was gone. He slammed the drawer shut and then ripped it out. Banged the drawer shut. Pulled it open. Slammed it—Mrs. Burr yelled,

"Stop that noise, Ray Martinez, stop it this instant!" Ray opened the drawer and violently closed it with a crash. Mrs. Burr was still yelling. "I'm going to count to three, only once. I'm starting to count . . ."

Ray looked inside the drawer, trying to calm himself. He couldn't make any more noise. Or John Henry would be up, and Mrs. Burr's voice had that crazy, wild sound. That's better. Ray was feeling better, looking into the drawer. He could get another pen. That's what he would do. And put it right there, up front so he could see it, and it would roll when he opened and closed the drawer. And everything would be back where it's supposed to be. The pen and his pocket watch with the broken stem. And his radio.

Ray arranged the top drawer every night. The radio next to the watch. And against the side of the drawer the "important papers" bound together by a rubber band. And way in back of the drawer a black jewel box. A miniature ballet dancer turned in a crippled pirouette as Ray lifted the lid to the jewel box and inspected its wealth. There were extra D batteries next to a Muni transfer, a note pad full of lines and circles, and the prize pearl necklace he'd found one day at the Ferry Building. But the real treasure was way back in the drawer under the box. No one knew he had this—not even Mrs. Burr.

Ray carefully removed the tattered magazine cover. Unfolded it. Pressed it out on the top of the bureau. Moved his fingers over the image of Elvis Presley getting an FBI badge from President Nixon. Ray studied Elvis, then looked at himself in the mirror. They were look-alikes.

Ray's top drawer was much like his life. His routine. Ray had his daily places and friends to see. This was what he called his work. "You know, I've got this job to see my friends, 'cause if I don't, you see, they won't be there." So his work was the same each day regardless of the weather or his physical condition or if he were a millionaire.

Early each morning Ray left Mrs. Burr's on Steiner Street and walked two blocks to Haight Street. Each

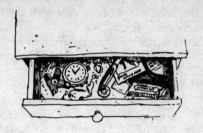

morning went like this: On Haight Street, he stopped to say good morning to Letty. Letty owned and operated Woolrite's Stationery and Fabric Store. She was always doing the morning sweeping of the street and talking about how the neighborhood was going to recover after the drug scene. "All those boarded-up stores, you'll see, are going to come to life," she'd say. Ray always agreed. On occasions, Letty would let him sweep while she stood there glaring up and down the street with her hands on her hips—like the mayor of a bombed-out city.

Farther down the street, Ray lingered at the window of the Donut Shop. A tall skinny man with a ponytail peered with equal intensity from his perch on a stool inside. The glass played its usual early-morning trick. Both men strained to see the other but saw their own reflection. Ray laughed at the sight of Elvis Presley with a ponytail. And the man inside studied the reflection of an ex-Digger and trumpet player for the Mime Troupe suddenly wearing the pompadour wave of dear Elvis. Both men shook their heads as they did every morning. Harold came out of the store and with a ready grin handed Ray a doughnut. It was Ray's favorite kind. Old-fashioned chocolate. He bowed in appreciation. A practiced ritual. And Harold gave his customary "Take care, Elvis." Ray waved good-bye, and Harold saluted with a fist in the air. Ray imitated the fisted salute. Harold smiled. Ray liked to see smiles.

The end of Haight Street spilled down Hippie Hill into Golden Gate Park. Hippie Hill was a grass slide that separated the hard edges of the city with the invitations of a primeval forest. The air was heavy with the perfume of marijuana and incense. Congo drummers stood like a picket fence, giving cadence to the young couple making love behind the lace of an acacia. Dancers with snake bodies nodded as Ray passed. His was a familiar pilgrimage. Ray quickened his pace, anticipating the comfortable openness of the Children's Playground. The morning sun glanced off the red stone castle that had been built as a place for mothers to nurse their children. With the morning sunlight, crenelated carvings came to life. Parapets and carved creatures opened their stone eyes. The pounding drums and tamborine chatter gave way to calliope whistles and grunts as the merry-go-round called to the children. Crystals of light spun in the air as ornamental stallions, lions, and zebras began their never-ending pursuit. Each time he passed, the lion lifted his paw and winked.

A sweeping curve of sun-warmed benches faced the carousel and the stone fortress. This is where Raymond sat in the morning with his friends the Rogers. They would be in their usual place at the end of their usual bench, wearing their glow knit caps, enjoying the comfort of this hollow, with the merry-go-round slowly turning and the children always stopping to say hello, only to be dragged away by nervous parents. This was their place, had been for as long as anyone could remember. This was the place of swings, painted horses, and Ray's friend Jake.

Jake was a police horse. Everyone knew Jake. The hippies, the children, the merchants, everyone. Jake was a giant with warm mirror eyes crowned by great curved lashes. The sound of his leather harness squeaked with the movement of each metaled hoof. Ray talked and petted Jake like this every morning. "Hello, horse, it's me Raymond Martinez, you want to give me a ride, like Elvis Presley, horse?" The officer sitting astride Jake shook his head sideways. It didn't matter. Ray wasn't talking to the policeman; he was talking to Jake. "Hello, horse," Ray whispered. "Willie Mays hit six hundred and forty-six home runs against Cincinnati in one game, Larry over there he listens to games like me." Ray chuckled. He was about to tell Jake the joke he played on the horse every day. "Do you like ice cream?" Ray laughed at his own joke. Then he pulled from his pocket a half-eaten doughnut. Jake was waiting for the doughnut.

Ray opened his hand flat, showing the chocolate treat. Jake's tongue was wet and effective. One slap of the tongue around the metal bit and the doughnut was gone. Jake tossed his head back in appreciation. He liked chocolate doughnuts, Ray took this as a nod good-bye. Ray looked up at the policeman. He admired that bright badge. Elvis Presley has a badge like that. And a horse. Someday he'd ride a horse and get a badge. Maybe. He knew a lot about horses. What they eat and what they like. He'd take good care of his horse.

A harmonic waltz carried the winking lion on its course and graced the movement of children at play and the clopping sound of Jake prancing over to the bocci-ball courts. It was a good place, this sunny corner of the park. If you closed your eyes, you could hear children laughing and shouting. Ray liked that sound. It was like the clanking of a cable-car bell.

There were other places Ray visited each day. The Ferry Building. The bathroom at Glide Memorial Church. The fountain at city hall. Each place had its daily opera of greetings and farewells between friends.

A Simple Request

December 16, 1971

Interruptions in Ray's universe of routine often come in the form of a simple request. For Raymond, any request is a command that must be obeyed. "Hey, man, you got some change you can give me?" a panhandler on the street asks. And Ray gladly gives this stranger all the money in his pocket. He does it without hesitation, mental gymnastics, or moral judgment. Someone has asked him for something, and he wants to comply. Wants to be helpful. Wants to do what is right. Wants to be liked.

Which can often send Raymond into a dangerous situation. Or a situation he cannot figure a way out of. The thing is, if you ask Ray to do something, you must also hang around to tell him how to finish it. For Raymond, a simple request like passing out candy canes can have unforeseen consequences. And tragedy.

"Raymond, you're just the person I wanted to see!" Letty was smiling and studying Ray. Yes, he was perfect, she thought. Just the right size. And everyone knows Ray. The other merchants all like him. Hell, he's always going into their stores, waiting for a handout. This way he can repay all that generosity. I don't know how many pencils and pens I've given him. And besides, there is no one else. She had considered wearing the costume herself, but then she'd have to close the store. And closing your store is not a great idea when the Haight-Ashbury Merchants Association, of which she is president, had planned this big Christmas party. The event was her idea. A parade of children led by Rudolph the Red-Nosed Reindeer down Haight Street and into the meadow next to the merry-go-round for a neighborhood party. The merchants purchased five hundred candy canes wrapped in silver and gold foil. And provided two hundred plastic ornaments containing prizes and discounts for the holiday shoppers. The giveaway prizes included a dozen doughnuts from the Donut Shop, a water pipe from the Head Store, a Handyman set of screwdrivers from Haight Hardware, free legal counseling from the 409 House, fifty percent off on the upholstery of your old couch—make it look like new—from the Used Furniture Palace, and an album of your choice from Light and Sound Records. . . .

Letty had worked hard on the parade and party. It was one more effort on her part to bring more commerce and nice families into the Haight. She involved everyone she knew in this effort. The Free Clinic was providing monitors in case someone played around with the candy. (White dope had replaced acid as the favorite street drug, but there was always the chance that some nut would lace the candy to "turn on the kids.") Following the parade, the parents at the Haight-Ashbury Cooperative Nursery School agreed to put on a Christmas puppet show. And the Angels of Light, a group of bearded men who enjoyed being women, volunteered to entertain with a cabaret show that would be followed by Christmas carols. They had connections to get the Jefferson Airplane sound equipment. White Punks on Dope, a political group that worked out of a neighborhood Baptist church, secured the parade permit and reserved the meadow. The 409 House printed flyers and distributed them door to door throughout the neighborhood.

Everything had worked out as planned except for this one problem. Someone had forgotten to enlist Santa's reindeer. The costume was rented and hanging in the storeroom of Letty's store; there just wasn't anyone available for the role. Anyone, that is, until Raymond took his early-morning walk and stopped to talk with Letty. Ray was hoping she might ask him to sweep the street when Letty explained her plan. "Raymond, you're just the person I wanted to see!" Ray smiled, expecting to be handed the broom. His outstretched hand received not a broom but Letty's firm handshake. She grasped Ray's hand and shook it wildly. "Yes, you're perfect. I hereby declare that you are this year's, actually this is our first annual, that you are the Haight-Ashbury's honorary reindeer—Rudolph the Red-Nosed Reindeer!" Ray stood perfectly still except for his hand and arm, which were levering up and down in a robust congratulatory handshake.

Letty was still talking. "Good, then you'll do it. I was worried there for a minute." Noticing Ray's perplexed look, Letty repeated what she thought was a question and what Ray heard as an order. "You will do it, won't you? I mean it will be easy, just walk down the street and lead the kids to the park, that's where the gifts will be given out and the party begins. The parade starts here at nine o'clock, and the party starts at ten. Then the puppet show. You can help Ed, you know Ed, he runs the Haight-Ashbury Neighborhood, oh, what's that, you know, H-A-N-C, he's going to introduce the puppet show, kinda serve as a master of ceremonies. . . ." Once Letty started, it was hard to stop her. So Ray stood quietly, and tried to listen. "Everything is ready. It's going to be a wonderful parade, we've even invited Mayor Alioto, but I, oh, that doesn't matter, the kids they all know you. I don't know why I didn't think of you for this . . ."

Letty ushered Ray into the storeroom of Woolrite's. Ray was excited and pleased to help his friend. And this was important. To be Rudolph the Red-Nosed Reindeer. Help make all the children happy. Give them presents. Walk them over the meadow next to the playground. Yes, he could do it. It was a real job. Better than sweeping for Letty or washing the window at the Donut Shop. This was important. He had to do things just right. It was important not to disappoint Letty or the children. Maybe he could even take some candy home. That's right. It would be nice if he worked. Then he could take some candy for Mrs. Burr and himself.

The storeroom was a confined space where cardboard boxes mated and had little boxes. Piles of boxes opened and closed their flap mouths as Ray struggled to put on the reindeer costume. Getting dressed was not one of Ray's easier accomplishments. So he tried to wear the same clothes every day. And he tried to put them on the same way: first his socks and then his shoes. The shoes were the biggest problem. It was tying the knots that confused him. His solution was to twist the shoe-string as tight as possible and then stick the braided and curled string into his shoe under a momentarily elevated heel. Then step down, hoping to trap the shoestring. The reindeer shoes were two huge balls of fur. Ray didn't want to risk taking his shoes off, so he jammed them into the slipperlike opening. It worked! Ray had pink reindeer feet. Ray stroked the furry feet and felt satisfied.

Letty impatiently yelled, "Are you all right in there? Do you need any help?" Raymond stuck one furry foot out the curtain entrance to the storeroom and pronounced happily, "I have the feet, see."

"Good," came a faint reply. "It's almost time to start . . ."

Ray didn't hear the remainder of Letty's comment. He was busy looking at the body of the costume. It hung on a hanger like some skinned animal. Ray had never seen anything like this. There were no pants. No shirt. Everything was sorta put together. There was a row of buttons. He was glad there were no zippers.

Raymond could handle buttons. He never did understand zippers. I mean how to start them. And if they went off track, well, that's the way they stayed. Since all his pants had zippers, he had to be extra careful never to pull at them or let them come unfastened. With pants, Ray wriggled into and out of them with the zipper held in one hand and always zipped close to the uppermost limit. Of course, exactly what he feared usually happened. The zipper would pull off its tracks. One day Mrs. Burr had given Ray a safety pin that he could use to fasten his pants. And the pin was a curse, too. It always sprang out of his pinching fingers or stuck him or, successfully closed, served only to open his fly to humiliating comments and more frustration. The pink costume in front of him had a pin at the neck opening.

Ray squeezed the pin, and it flew open. It slipped away from his grasp, landing on the floor. As Ray bent to retrieve the pin, he unleashed an avalanche of boxes. Picking up the fallen boxes and trying to pile them out of the way caused other boxes to tumble. Not only had he lost the pin, but now his feet were lost under boxes. Each step brought further confusion. "Are you all right in there?" Letty asked. "Is everything—did you find the costume?"

Ray answered, "I lost the pin, I can't see it."

Letty didn't catch his concern. "Rudolf's head is under the sink, the parade's about to start, can you hurry a bit?"

Ray carefully picked up the fallen boxes and piled them in precarious pyramids. Once the debris was finally cleared, he swept his hand across the floor surface. The pin was missing! Ray frantically searched the soft reindeer hoofs and the floor. Still no pin. In frustration, he stood up and angrily closed the cabinet door above the sink. Seeing himself in the cabinet mirror, he realized he needed scolding. "You lost the pin, where's the pin, you stupid, stupid, you lose everything, I ought to kill you!" Ray pounded his fist into the edge of the sink. "Why can't I do things right, I ought to kill you!"

Trembling and close to tears, Ray returned to his hands and knees and swept the floor with wider and wider strokes of his hand. Still no pin. He had to find it! Letty would be angry. Having searched the same area over and over, Ray turned to look under the sink. He almost cracked his head at the sight that greeted him. It was the giant head of a reindeer. With treelike antlers and bulging eyes that seemed to follow his every move. When Ray lifted the hollow mask, he was surprised at how light it felt. Then, under a floppy antler, Ray's fingers touched the safety pin. Ray took a deep breath. He wanted to yell but didn't. Fearing the pin's escape, he stood up and carefully placed it deep inside his pants pocket. Ray's confidence soared. He had found the pin. Looked in the right place and everything. Now all he had to do was put on the costume.

Ray crammed one foot into a leg. With one foot stuck halfway down the pants leg, he tried to hop but stumbled backward instead. The fall propelled the furry foot through the pants leg. Ray surveyed the situation and congratulated himself. Now can I do that again? Ray was about to throw himself backward when the second foot simply slid through the pants leg. He had unconsciously pointed his reindeer slipper, and his foot slipped forward. Ray didn't know why this second effort was so easy. He didn't stop to think about it. The costume was almost on.

Ray hiked the pants up and tried to thrust his arms into their slots. The upward jerk of fabric held him suspended. Trapped. He couldn't force his arms through their openings, and he couldn't retract them. If the boxes that surrounded him had been an Indian war party, they'd have found Rudolph the Red-Nosed Reindeer trying to surrender to them. But before they could celebrate, their captive tried one last escape. Ray was angry. Mad at what always confounded him. He wrestled the resisting fabric one way, then another. Like Houdini, he bucked sideways and stamped his feet. Twisted in a full spin. Then bowed his body at the waist, trying to invert his arms and throw off the costume. There was a ripping sound as Ray's arms shot forward from their prison.

Letty threw back the curtain and observed the headless reindeer. "Well, well, good, you look almost ready. Where did you hang your clothes?" Ray couldn't answer. The battle of dressing was never won. He was still pulling one hand through the cuff when Letty spoke again. "Do you want to use the locker for your clothes—they'll be safe there."

Raymond didn't answer. And after another look at her frazzled reindeer, Letty decided to help him put on the mittens and headpiece. She buttoned up the front of the costume and placed the papier-mâché ball over Ray's head. She tapped the side of it and turned it about as one would fit a diving helmet on the head of a deep-sea diver. Letty stood back and asked Ray if he could see. Ray's reply was muffled and inaudible. Letty asked again, "Can you see?" Ray nodded the cumbersome head.

Actually, the only way Ray could see was by putting his thumbs under the edge of the wobbling headpiece and pushing it slightly backward. This positioning of the massive head allowed him to squint through the pinhole opening in the eyes. Given the giant cheeks of the mask and the bulging eyes, the eyeholes were several inches away from Ray's face. It was easy to see the inside ribbing of the mask. But the world outside seemed as if viewed through the wrong end of binoculars. Everything was in miniature. And everything jumped with the slightest movement of the headpiece. One second, Ray was looking at a miniature version of Letty's face; the next, he was looking upon a row of boxes. Every adjustment Ray made to steady the head seemed to set off a gyroscopic tilting of the giant antlers, and this meant that his eyeholes got knocked askew, and this meant he had to make another adjustment. And this set off another tilt. . . .

A Request That Has No End

Letty was pushing Ray toward the door, complaining, "Don't forget to pass out these candy canes along the way, here, take this basket, Ed will give you some more at the entrance to the park—are you all right in there, can you see?" Ray walked straight into a display rack of Paper Mate pens. And when he turned around and tried to bend over, his antler karate chopped the side of the cash register. The money drawer sprang open, sending a shiver through Letty. "All right, all right, everything is all right, let's just get you on your way, no, no, don't pick up anything, everything is all right."

Everything was not all right. Letty gave Ray a final push out the doorway. Ray was standing alone in the middle of the sidewalk. He tilted the monstrous head in an attempt to see. Ray swiveled his head up the street and down. There were no children to be seen. Not a parent. Much less a parade.

Letty yelled from inside the store. "Go on, the children will follow you . . ." Ray nodded and started off down the street. Perhaps the children were waiting for him. Maybe at the Donut Shop. Each step set the top-heavy headpiece and antlers gyrating. The rolling combined with the intense concentration needed to see made Ray seasick. He couldn't get sick. Not now. This was an important job. Letty has asked him to be the reindeer. Lead the parade. For all the merchants and children. Perspiration welled into Ray's eyes. It made them sting. Ray swept his mitten upward to wipe his eyes. The swinging hand clumped into the side of the papier-mâché head. Once again, Ray couldn't see.

"Hey, you, are you the holy reindeer?" Ray turned

toward the question, tilted the head slightly, and blinked his eyes. "Far out, I mean, right here, like this is the moment of my life and the answer is yes, I will follow you, wherever . . ." Ray scanned the face of a red-cheeked girl. She must have been about fourteen. She sprinkled a handful of sparkling dust into the air and curtsied. Ray lost her. She'd dropped below the rim of his vision. When he looked downward, he saw her bare feet, then, above that, a long white lacy dress, and then an innocent face graced by a halo of mistletoe. Her face was aglow with streaks of color. Stars and moons painted around her eyes caused her features to blend with the psychedelic posters that pulsated behind her.

Ray waved a greeting with a mitten. "Hello," he said cheerfully. The sound reverberated inside the hollow mask. The girl in the lace dress returned the greeting by dancing gaily around the pink reindeer. Ray couldn't follow her Isadora movements. He saw a hand, then a swirl of a skirt and snowlike crystals falling all about him.

This color and flashing movement followed him down the street. Farther up the block, two winos lunged at him from their doorway homes. They crashed clumsily into Ray and his bride. Candy canes went every way. Ray clutched the now-half-empty basket in both mittens, like a fullback covering a football, and started running. The bouncing headpiece jolted against his shoulder. The street ahead of him flickered like the chase scene in a silent movie. Ray closed his eyes and ran. He stumbled over a curb and knocked over a newspaper rack. Glanced off a telephone pole. Still he ran, clutching the basket. He was afraid to stop or take off the headpiece. Afraid to stop. Make Letty angry.

At the corner of Haight and Stanyan, Ray felt himself being handled to a stop. Hands pushed at him, grabbed at his tail, patted his mittens. Ray squinted out the tiny opening. He was surrounded by children. They were jumping up and down with excitement, yelling greetings to Rudolph, asking for candy. The embrace of children cushioned and slowed Ray. The place where the parade was to end became the place where the parade began.

Through his eye slots, Ray saw smiling parents, bashful babies, and frenzied children. It was strange. Ray seemed to see clearly. It was as if the beauty of what he saw determined the clarity of his vision. Ray was happy. Children squeezed his hand. Wanted to walk with him. He saw their look of wonderment. Heard their peals of delight. Children spun in the air like tops. Younger eyes played tag with the reindeer's gaze. They looked first away and then quickly returned to confirm that this apparition was real. Ray tilted his head in greeting. Small faces smiled and looked away to continue the game. The parents were smiling, too, and talking to the reindeer with the red nose. "Hello, Rudolph, is that you, Ed, how's it feel in there, great job—cute little tail you have there. . . ."

The rush of families waded across Stanyan Street, pushing and pulling at the reindeer with the wobbling horns and bushy tail. The group entered the park, singing. At first, Ray couldn't decipher what everyone was voicing, but in time it became clear. He joined in. Lifting his feet extra high. Bobbing his body to the cadence.

> *Rudolph the red-nosed reindeer*
> *Had a very shiny nose,*
> *And if you ever saw it,*
> *You would even say it glows.*
> *All of the other reindeer . . .*

The singing parade swirled past the congo drummers and the sad voyagers using the park as their temporary home. Draping their sleeping bags and blankets around them, they stood and officially greeted the parade like royalty reviewing a passing army. They were glad to share the park with brothers and sisters of Santana and Joplin. Children of the Grateful Dead. In automatic fashion, they followed the procession.

At the meadow next to the playground, merchants

dressed in Santa Claus caps and white beards directed the throng to the puppet stage. Small children were guided to places close to the stage. Older children and adults closed in behind them. The crowd was still serenading itself. Only a group of laughing parents had broken out in a boisterous version of "Jingle Bells."

In all of this, Ray was turned first one way, then another. He had become completely exhausted by the insistence of the parents, with their Polaroids, asking for just one more pose. He could no longer hold his arms up and steady the wobbly head. The sour taste of morning Cheerios rose in his throat, flooding the back of his mouth. He swallowed vomit down. Then fought its next upsurge. He spun about blindly. Following the pull of children's hands and the prodding of adult voices for just one more picture before the puppet show started. He was desperately thirsty but dared not remove the mask. His legs were shaking. Still he continued, determined not to disappoint the children or Letty, who had told him to lead the parade. It did not occur to Ray that the parade was over or that he could sit down or duck into the puppet tent. He was obeying a request that had no end.

So as the puppet show and cabaret entertainment ended, Ray spontaneously moved to please an unseen child or invisible adult. He waved and bowed. Shook hands. Danced. Fought to keep balance while older children chased around him and pulled his tail. Stood as still as possible as urine ran down his inner pants leg and soaked into his clothing. Curled his toes to keep the flopping slippers attached to his feet. And tried to clean his sticky mittens by rubbing them against a tree. Ray did everything in his power to follow a simple request.

Several hours had passed before Raymond realized that the crowd was finally drifting home. San Francisco's winter fog was clearing the park of revelers. It billowed up from the ocean like a vaporous wave, covering first the sky, then the earth itself. The Christmas party had been over for quite a while. The stage, with its rainbow banners and wreaths of evergreen, disappeared. The balloon salesman in the elf suit had followed his balloons toward the Panhandle and a cup of warm soup given by the Diggers. The children, with their ringing voices and clicking white shoes, were nowhere in sight. Wisps of fog shrouded Ray in comforting coolness. He tilted the headpiece and let the dampness rush into the steamy mask. He stuck out his tongue in a doglike pant. Glad for the relief. He bent over, trying to gain strength and decide what to do next. No one had told him exactly what to do. He was to lead the parade and be Rudolph the Red-Nosed Reindeer, but for how long? And what to do after all the people were gone and it was dark?

Ray couldn't decide. The one thing he was sure about was keeping on the costume and waiting for Letty. Surely she would come and tell him when his job was over. To pass the time, he went over to his favorite bench next to the merry-go-round. And then to the swings. It was early evening, and the only people in the park were curling into sleeping bags or scurrying for the lighted avenues. The gray blanket of fog was now giving way to the darkness. As if to stay on center stage for a few more moments, the fog swirled insistently around the ornamental lamps, gathering and reflecting particles of light, holding off the end of day.

Ray swung back and forth. He sang "Love Me Tender" to himself as he crisscrossed the wet air. Closing his eyes, he felt antlers sagging back and forth with each thrust of the swing. Then he stopped singing. And listened for the steady clank of the swing. Clank, clank, clank.

The fog surrounded the solitary figure with a delicate embroidery. Trees of green evaporated into gray and then melted out of sight. The carousel's bright colors and dancing zebras faded. A pink reindeer on his swing was hidden by the white gloves of this wet magician. But it was darkness that performed the final fusing of light, the ultimate illusion. Then all that remained was a repeated sound. Clank, clank, clank.

The noise of the swing drew more than the night. Ray still couldn't see out of the mask, but he knew someone was approaching. Perhaps it was Letty. He slowed the swing by dragging his feet. Before it stopped, some-one from behind grabbed Raymond by the neck and yanked him to the ground. The tanbark cushioned Ray's fall but not the rain of fists that plowed into his stomach and groin. Ray tried to curl up, but someone kicked the head of the costume as if it were a football. The force of the blows sent the head flying off Ray's shoulders. Which meant that Ray could see. There were four or five of them. Men with letter jackets. Fraternity brothers on a romp through Hippie Land. They were laughing. Throwing beer cans at the crumpled reindeer.

"Look at this, this ain't no hippie, it's a reindeer!" "Let's cut off his ears!" Raymond smelled armpits and the sour breath of beer.

One of the drunks took a pair of scissors from a back pocket and snapped them over Ray's face. "There's no hair, man, look, he's a greaser—hey, greaser, what you doin' here in Hippie Land wearin' that—he must be a hippie—hell, cut off somethin'—that's what we're here for!" At that, the gang yelled something, and each one flashed a pair of scissors into the cold air.

Enjoying their torment, they cut off the cotton-ball buttons that held up the reindeer suit. They laughed and shouted with each severed button. Then they wrenched the top of the suit over Ray's shoulders and started to pull the costume off his hips. When they saw that Raymond was wearing a set of clothes under the costume, they snapped their scissors with gleeful anticipation. Then they realized something else. And all together they reeled back from their prey. Ray's pants were soaked in urine and reeked from a bowel movement. The clean-cut middle-class attackers stiffened in pain. "Oh, hey, I can't handle this, this guy stinks—what's with this guy—you a basket case or something?"

Unwilling to dirty their hands, the notorious S Gang was content to stomp their victim. They kicked a writhing and sobbing Raymond until the thumps pro-duced a hollow moan. Content that they had saved the world for clean living and the American Way, they raced off to find other long-haired aliens and reindeer.

Ray's body squeezed open and closed like an accordion. Each movement brought a spasm of pain. A dull cry. Each breath fought its way to his lungs and then retreated in a bloody cough. Worried about the buttons, Ray spread out his arms and spread the puffs of cotton toward the gaping front of his costume. He slowly placed each cotton button into his pants pocket. Each change of position started a new ache.

Pinning the costume with a clenched fist, Raymond reached for the papier-mâché head. He traced the nose and puffy cheeks with his fingertips. Then followed the contour of each felt antler. And the bulge of the huge eyes. Everything seemed intact. He was happy. Nothing serious had happened to the costume. He lifted the awkward headpiece and stuck his head into the opening. The papier-mâché ball settled onto his shoulders. Now the tiny eyeholes were partly closed with dirt. It didn't matter. With one arm, Raymond pulled himself back onto the canvas seat of the swing. And gave a gentle push with his feet. He swung suspended in the night air. Waiting for another simple request. Waiting to be helpful. To do what is right. To be liked.

Clank.

Clank.

Clank.

Holy Ghosts

<u>December 17, 1971</u>

It was almost midnight when Raymond, still wearing his reindeer outfit, found his way home. Ray knew that Mrs. Burr was still up because the television set was illuminating the front room. And he could hear the dogs barking as he climbed the wooden stairs. Ray was afraid of the dogs. He didn't like their loud noises and always feared they were going to bite him.

Ray cautiously entered the darkened living room. The house had a musty odor of old age and dereliction. Gas fixtures that once flattered this Victorian lady still protruded from the walls like brass coat hooks. They twisted from their mountings and dangled like broken teeth from the patterned wallpaper. Parquet flooring that had once been the pride of an Italian carpenter was now covered with linoleum merchants' bargains. And the wainscoting was painted a lipstick red.

The television's blue light etched the face of Mrs. Burr. As always, she sat in the same corner of a large plastic-covered "silk shantung" couch. Sitting in the same spot was her way, as she said, of "keeping it like new." Of course the spot where she sat had caved in with use and was stained from food spills—an oil slick on a sea of orange silk. The television images played on her stoic face as Raymond took a step into the room.

Ray had forgotten that he was a pink reindeer. The large dogs rose from their sleeping spots alongside the couch and sauntered toward the strange horned creature. They poked their noses under the pants cuff of the costume and sniffed. The small dogs started yapping and doing a dog version of kung fu. They bounded to one side, then another. Barked and retreated. Rushed forward to test. Ray took off the spiked headpiece and waved it at the palace guard like a tamer holding off a circus lion with a chair.

Ray was bursting with things to say. He wanted to show Mrs. Burr his costume. And ask her about so many things. All of his concerns gushed out at once. "I was the holy reindeer, and these men, they beat me up, kicked me, look at this here—Letty asked me, asked me to be this reindeer for her and the children, there were no children. I looked and there were no children. I saw Santa Claus. I was his favorite reindeer, he said that, Letty didn't come so I went swinging and these guys kicked me. Right here!" Ray pointed to the dent in the side of the Rudolph's head. Then continued speaking and moving his free hand like a policeman directing rush-hour traffic.

"I was Rudolph the Red-Nosed Reindeer. We all sang, the children and everybody, crossing the street, we sang 'Rudolph the Red-Nosed Reindeer had a very shiny nose.' And everything. I had candy canes, Letty gave me candy canes to give to the children. These guys kicked me right here and punched me. Letty didn't do it, she wasn't there with me. I lost the candy canes." Ray was talking to Mrs. Burr, but only the dogs were listening. And once they recognized a familiar voice and a familiar face, they returned with Mrs. Burr to the Johnny Carson show.

Mrs. Burr sat impassively, like a queen hearing the tedious complaints of yet one more subject. As usual, she was wearing a floral print dress that draped over her excess flesh. Her pursed red lips, penciled eye makeup, and lacquered white hair gave her the appearance of a china doll. She wore this garish makeup and starched appearance to mask her sixty years. Her eyes seemed to have a split personality. They darted about nervously, then would fix on a single object—usually something to eat. They seemed like burning coals behind a wax wall. And there was something else. The fingers of Mrs. Burr's right hand twitched every time Ray spoke. When he stopped, they stopped. The eyes and the fingers worked together like some magnetic force. Mrs. Burr didn't have to speak. Her coiled expression and ticking fingers excluded interruption as surely as any word or act. Raymond's words, questions, and prideful boasts fell to the floor, then crawled for cover. Mrs. Burr reached for another chocolate. She seemed hypnotized by Ed McMahon and the Alpo commercial.

Actually, Mrs. Burr seldom talked with the boarders that lived upstairs. She created her own world, and they were mere satellites. She tried to minimize these intrusions in her life. Oh, she liked the three hundred and four hundred dollars she was paid each month to "take care" of each boarder; but as far as actual care, well, that was the job of her stepson John Henry Butler. She and Butler were always fighting over "the money" and his complaint about "the work" and "the promises" she made to him.

Butler did most of what he called "the dredges." There were four people living upstairs. Ray and the Rogers, along with an elderly woman that Raymond had only seen on occasion. Butler did the meals. Every morning at eight o'clock there was a loud bell that signaled that Ray and the others could go downstairs for breakfast. Breakfast was always the same. Cheerios and toast. After breakfast, you could watch television in the empty bedroom upstairs or go out for the day. Mrs. Burr preferred two types of clients—men, because they didn't get raped on the streets and cause lots of extra problems, and bedridden clients, because they couldn't make demands on your time. The Rogers were for Mrs. Burr a trial couple. She didn't like Mrs. Rogers. Mrs. Rogers talked too much. She refused eat to everything with a spoon. She wanted a knife and fork with dinner. And insisted on "ordering" those new TV dinners and Swanson pies, "since we always eat in the room with the television." And she liked butter, not margarine. And wanted her clothes returned.

John Henry Butler was responsible for clothes washing. Once a week, Butler came to each room and stuffed any dirty clothes he could find in a pillowcase. Butler sometimes let Ray go along for the washing. At the corner laundromat, Butler dumped everything into a washer and fed the machine a dime. If there was soap in the house, he took it along. If not, he washed without it. While the clothes washed, Butler played pinball across the street. Butler let Ray watch the washing machine and come and get him when the machine stopped. "They were a team," Butler said.

As for the returned clothes, well, Ray and Larry Rogers were always getting each other's stuff. And the two women simply received whatever came out of the bag. Jocelyn Rogers was the only one to claim that she knew "her" clothes and wanted "her" clothes. Butler solved that by letting her wash "her" clothes with "her" allowance money. Each resident got an allowance to spend any way they wanted. Ray got a dollar bill at breakfast at the start of the week. Sometimes Butler kept the dollar "to bet for Ray." Sometimes Ray would get to work for his dollar. Ray enjoyed "his work." He would wash the dishes and maybe go with Butler to get Kentucky Fried Chicken or shop for the Swansons that Mrs. Rogers liked. Butler hated to go shopping.

On one occasion, Ray got to clean the old lady's room. Ray had always thought there were two old ladies in the corner room, but there was only one. She was a frail birdlike figure who never came downstairs for breakfast or watched television. There were two beds in the room, and Ray helped Butler place clean sheets on the spare bed and then lift the drooling old lady from her soiled bed into the fresh one. In the transfer, her long fingernails curved like talons and picked at festering sores. On cleaning day, Butler would often just walk past the closed corner-room door rather than contend with the lifting and changing of bed sheets. Since Ray had never seen the old woman at breakfast or dinner, he didn't know when she ate. There were dirty dishes and empty glasses with sediment rings next to the bed, so she must have eaten sometime.

Ray and Butler were friends of a sort. Butler teased Ray a lot about "getting any" and about knowing where Ray hid his *Playboy* magazines. Ray kept them under his pillow, but they were always slipping from their hiding place and falling to the floor. Butler sometimes borrowed Ray's magazines and sometimes treated Ray to a beer. But Ray liked it best when Butler would come upstairs and just sit quietly and listen to the Giants or Forty-Niners. Ray considered Butler to be his best friend. Butler didn't have many other friends, or at least none that Ray ever saw.

One nice thing about Butler was that he preferred to be upstairs than downstairs. Except for breakfast in the kitchen, downstairs was off limits to the upstairs people. They could only come down when the bell rang. Downstairs was the residence of Mrs. Burr and her pets. She had a bedroom in the parlor next to the living room. This room was like a museum of baroque furniture and carnival bric-a-brac. A large canopy bed with a dozen fringed pillows dominated the center of the room. And a Chinese screen of mahogany and silk and an ornate dressing table were against the wall. A panoply of art-deco atomizers, cream jars, heart-shaped candy boxes, and bottles of perfume and cologne fought for a place on the dressing table and bureaus. In the corner, there were piles of movie magazines and old seventy-eight records.

At first glance, the room was a place of crystal and wondrous things, but upon closer observation, the room was simply dirty.

Mrs. Burr didn't move as Ray walked down the hallway tunnel to the stairs. She didn't raise a hand. Or scold. Or inquire. It was Butler's job to take care of the clients, and he was out someplace. As Ray passed, she followed him with one squidlike eye, then returned her attention to chee-chees and the start of the late-night movie.

Hurt and worried, Ray entered his room. His bruises were swelling, and his head throbbed. But the cut-off buttons drew his greatest concern. He didn't know what to do with the costume. And the buttons were cut off. He tried holding them in place on the front of the suit, but they didn't adhere as he hoped they might. The buttons—that was the big problem. Letty had given him the suit, and the buttons were off. What would she say and do? Raymond had been bad! Hurt the costume. Raymond was bad!

Ray knew what he had to do when he was bad. He'd done what he had to do over and over. God told him what to do. It was God's will. A priest dressed in a black robe had taken Ray's hand and told him about the fourteen stations of the cross. And the suffering of Jesus for our sins. Jesus carrying the cross. The veil. And the soldier that would not break the legs of Jesus. Nailing Jesus. Driving spikes through the palm of his hand. It was Ray's fault they nailed Jesus to the cross. And being bad, you had to suffer. There were candles to light. And Raymond put his hand into the fire. For Jesus. To be good. To do what was right. Suffer for Jesus. Take his place on the cross. Feel his pain. The nails driven into outstretched hands.

Ray had been bad, causing Jesus to die. He had killed Jesus. And he had been bad losing the buttons. They wouldn't go back on. Ray felt terrible. He didn't want to be bad. But he was bad. The priest said so. Then Ray had put his hand in the fire to show his love for Jesus, and the priest said he had given penance for all our sins. Shown his love for Jesus. Shared the pain of Jesus on the cross.

Ray's chant of sin and penitence repeated itself over and over, as it had done since he was a young child attending his first lenten service. Ray reached under his bed and found the can of Sterno and the box of matches hidden there.

Ray placed the Sterno can on his bureau. Then slowly tore each match from its protective cover and arranged them into a pyre in the center of the Sterno. Suddenly, Ray realized he was wearing mittens. He stripped them off but didn't know where to put them. He tried stuffing them into his pants pocket. They didn't fit. Opening the top drawer, Ray surveyed his things—that was not the spot for his mittens. Pacing the room, Ray found just the right place. He carefully folded the mittens and shoved the pink mound under his bed in the space reserved for his matches.

Returning to the Sterno can, Ray struck a match and ignited the fuel. A bright orange flame licked at the oxygen and turned a hot blue. Ray put his hand high above the flame, feeling the escaping heat. He rocked back and forth on his heels. His face contorted. Eyes closing. Ray plunged his open palm into the blade of the flame. The seared skin released a pungent smell. Ray yelled in pain and yanked his hand free. He crumpled to the floor below the flame, clutching his blistered hand and crying, "I'm bad. Bad. I should kill myself. . . ."

For The Lady With A Lunch-Bag Hanky

December 19, 1971
Martinez, Raymond
#03-016-9657

Housing Suitability
  I've placed Mrs. Burr's board-and-care home under close scrutiny by the Health Department for the violation of sanitation codes and the lack of fire doors and emergency exits. Conferences with other workers indicate Mrs. Burr's operation to be marginal. There is no personal hygiene or recreation program offered clients. Clients have been found tied to their beds and chairs. (Mrs. Burr claims it's for their safety.) The home currently has only one working bathroom and no means for the washing and drying of clothing. (Mrs. Burr claims she will be purchasing a new washer and dryer.) It's only the increasing need for board-and-care operations due to the closing of state mental hospitals and lack of standards for licensing operators that has permitted Mrs. Burr to stay in operation.

Inheritance Issue
  I still question the advisability of letting Mrs. Burr's stepson John Henry Butler serve as the legal guardian for Ray. Butler has not returned my call regarding a requested list of Ray's assets and plans for a trust fund. Part of the problem is that if Ray's income exceeds twelve hundred dollars, he will not be able to receive ATD assistance.
  Attached is the decree of distribution for the estate of Ray's father. According to this document, filed July 2, 1965, Ray should be entitled to some stock and

half interest in a house valued in 1965 at $19,500. The stepmother reports that she wishes to sell the house but does not plan to give Ray any money from this sale. Mr. Wilkins, the attorney for Ray and his guardian, assures me that Ray will be protected. Mr. Wilkins was quite agitated "that this office would check up on him," as he thinks our office "abrogated its responsibility in this matter" and "Mr. Butler is now the legal guardian!" When I asked Mr. Wilkins to have Butler contact me, he insisted that "all communications on this matter should go through his office!"

According to workers in the office, Butler does not seem to have ever had a job outside of odd jobs for his mother. He is only a few years older than Ray, and it's hard for me to comprehend his effectiveness as a guardian. I've been asked by at least one worker to check whether Butler has a criminal record.

Plan of Action

My main concern is to give Ray a chance to manage his own affairs. He needs to find placement in a sheltered workshop and participate in a recreational program. I plan to refer this case to J. B. Carver, supervisor, Unit 210, Eligibility Control and Fraud Investigation.

Croce-Carver 12/19/71

Miss Croce filled out her quarterly reports as she had been doing for seventeen years. But now she was working on her own time. That's the only way her reports would get done. Work was becoming a race. Only this race never ended. The finish line kept moving farther and farther away. Her case-load limit of 60 in 1970 had been "temporarily extended" to 75—then 115. Now it was temporarily just two more. Temporarily 117. She felt she was spending all her time shuffling papers. And to make matters worse, there was the transition of services to the Feds.

The Feds were taking over the distribution of checks

and eligibility verification. Accordingly, half the local Department of Social Services office was being "phased out." For Miss Croce, this meant that a working force of twenty-one service units with six workers per unit was being trimmed to five units with a total personnel of 73 workers. No one knew who was going to keep their job. Or how seniority would be applied if there were layoffs. Supervisors, fearing this loss of staff and their respective positions, requested staff to start proposal writing. It was very frustrating. No one knew how to write proposals for funding, who to write to, or what to possibly ask for. Staff was memoed to write proposals to the Feds for "innovative projects" such as escort services, client councils on consumer affairs, and nutritional clinics. For Miss Croce and others in her office, it all seemed like such a mess—the Feds were taking the job they knew how to perform well and asking them to start projects they knew nothing about!

To heighten this confusion, there was the "immediate transfer of records." The Feds wanted all the eligibility files. Each worker was trying to keep up with the flood of new aid requests and at the same time begin the task of packing files for shipment to Alabama or Washington, D.C. Dates for the removal of all files were posted on office day boards. The dates for the shipment of files and the addresses changed weekly. Foremost boxes, stuffed full of files, were placed out in the halls like garbage cans. Only to be retrieved and stacked in office corners. Of course, the files buried in these boxes contained the vital information needed by workers to process the transfers. So boxes were always being opened to get vital case information and then sealed, only to be opened again. Lots of workers started duplicating files or tried to submit to memory the pertinent details of their case load. Staff members were walking around like nuns with their worry beads. Only instead of Hail Marys, you'd hear the mumbled repeating of clients' names, phone numbers, and dates.

This overload was having its crushing effects. Some

workers just stopped. They'd reach a point of frustration and exhaustion and just stop. They'd sit at their desks all day—looking at the same file. Others became frantic with anxiety. They'd rush to get some lost file, rush to meet a client, rush to submit a revised proposal, rush to eat, rush to get some lost file, rush to meet a client, rush . . .

The sadness that shrouded everyone was the loss of contact with people who ought to have been served. The loss of rewards for doing your work. The loss of feeling responsible. A sudden awareness came to everyone in Miss Croce's office that they were neither needed nor wanted. Once that feeling began to creep into the job, the office, which used to crackle with rumors, gossip, and humor, now soured with misplaced anger. They complained over and over. "I'm making $724 a month for all this crap, and my clients get $439 for sitting on their ass." The love-hate relationship that is inevitable in service jobs began to tilt toward hatred. Workers began to hate their job. Hate their clients. And hate themselves.

Miss Croce wasn't immune to this poison. In some ways, she felt the pressure more than others. She prided herself on neatness, efficiency, punctuality, and overall concern. During the year, she had missed work only once and had never been late. In December 1971, Miss Croce was absent from work on three occasions and was late to work once. It aggravated her to put her Foremost file boxes out in the hall for a pickup that never came. And she just never had enough time for herself or her clients. Finally, one morning, she pulled the covers over her head and just stayed in bed. Didn't read or watch TV and wasn't sick. She just lay there.

We Wish You A Merry Christmas

December 24, 1971

Larry and Jocelyn Rogers clamored into Ray's room, excited by the prospect of putting up a Christmas tree. It had been twenty years since they decorated their own tree, and they were going to let Ray help them. "Especially," Jocelyn said, pointing to the bay window, "since you have Christmas lights here." Ray was delighted by all the commotion. He and Larry watched in awe as Jocelyn pulled a kitchen knife from her coat pocket and began prying the strands of lights from the nails that held the bulbs around the window. "Mrs. Burr's not going to like this," Ray worried out loud. "She's going to send John Henry up here . . ." Jocelyn didn't hesitate. Like always, she was a woman on a mission. And this particular crusade was to decorate a Christmas tree.

With a snap of the knife, the string of lights fell into Ray's hands. "Now hand me the loose end," Jocelyn commanded. Ray grabbed the plug end of the light strand and handed it to her. Holding the string of lights like the neck of a salami, Jocelyn hacked away with her knife until the plug dropped to the door. "See this here," she said. "This is the wire. It's still good wire, 'cause you can see its gold color. Now all we gotta do is put the lights around Larry and finish up with decorating. And we have a first-rate Christmas tree."

As per Jocelyn's exact instructions, Larry stood with arms outstretched, and Ray draped the string of lights around him, tucking colored bulbs into pockets, weaving the strand of electric bulbs around Larry's neck and jacket. All the while, Jocelyn was busy skinning the protective coating off the wire where the plug had been and wadding the exposed wire into a ball. She was giggling with anticipation. "This is going to be the best Christmas tree yet. We're sure going to show this Ray here a real, lights and everything Christmas tree, ain't that right, Larry!"

Larry and Jocelyn Rogers had known each other at Napa State Hospital. For twenty years, they had been friends on B Ward. During the previous year's massive release of patients, the discharge nurse couldn't find Jocelyn's records. So, in order to complete the necessary release form, she gave Jocelyn Larry's family name—Rogers. And on the form where it asked if Larry and Jocelyn were married, the nurse checked "yes." Larry and Jocelyn Rogers did not complain about this Paper Mate wedding. In fact, they themselves were not sure if they were man and wife, brother and sister, or just friends. It didn't matter to their way of thinking. They had been together for twenty years of confinement, and they were, as Jocelyn put it, "living now, together, forever."

Living in the now, together, forever, Larry and Jocelyn were both in their late sixties, although neither could tell you their birth date or exact age. Jocelyn was short and squat. Her gray hair sprang out from beneath her glow knit cap like a volcanic explosion. Natural ringlets of hair jiggled into the air every time she moved. And she was always moving. Moving to pick up a discarded pop bottle or a shiny piece of paper or an interesting rock. She stashed most of what she collected in the pockets or lining of her clothing. She always wore more than one pair of socks, more than one dress, more than one sweater, and a heavy tentlike coat. Each pocket bulged with its treasure of found objects. Jocelyn loved to trade these "things of hers" and help people on the street by offering them the Cheerios she stored in her coat pocket.

In the street life of the Haight, she didn't hesitate to enter any situation and had Cheerios to apply to every problem. Jocelyn joined in every civic event, from a local police bust to the free concerts in the park, where, on the periphery, she appeared like some paper-bag royalty. Of course, her aide-de-camp was Larry.

Larry Rogers was a silent witness to most of her activity. He hadn't given up on life; it was just easier to let Jocelyn eat the spinach in the family. If Jocelyn was like an overdressed pumpkin, he was like a scarecrow. He was tall and skinny, with arms and legs shooting far out of his plaid jacket and pants. Like Jocelyn, he wore an orange glow knit cap. It was the one thing everyone received upon their release from the hospital. Larry's cap covered coal-black hair that was Brylcreemed back and parted on one side. Like his mouth, it never moved. But Larry was content. He was happy to do whatever Jocelyn asked, even if it was to stand with his arms outstretched and pretend to be a Christmas tree.

"Now all we need is some fancy ornaments and some tinsel stuff," Jocelyn was explaining while reaching into an inside pocket of her coat. "This should—don't move Larry—this should do it." Jocelyn produced from her coat a beat-up roll of aluminum foil.

Ray was amazed. "I wish I had a coat like that."

Jocelyn didn't hear him; she was preoccupied with giving Ray instructions in tree decoration. "You pull out some of this here foil and then tear it into strips—

Larry hold still—that's it, pull it out and tear off a piece, good." Ray and Jocelyn played momentary tug-of-war with the foil.

Ray finally stepped on the unraveling sheet and ripped a piece skyward. "Well, that's a good way to do it," Jocelyn said.

Ray bubbled with enthusiasm. "Hey, this is all right, our, mine, too, a Christmas tree, right here, all right!"

Ray and Jocelyn frantically worked to tinsel the tree. Strips of metallic fringe were looped around Larry's arms, placed over his shoulders, and stuffed into his shirt collar and belt. With great fanfare, Jocelyn completed the final decoration by sticking metal strips under Larry's cap and letting the excess cover Larry's face. That did it. In the center of Ray's room stood a Christmas tree of shimmering tinsel and a string of colored lights. Actually, it looked like a rocket with an orange cone about to blast off. But to Ray and Jocelyn it was their Christmas tree, and it was perfect. The only thing that remained was to plug in the lights.

Jocelyn circled the quivering mass of metal and then spoke to the tree. "Larry, can you hear me? Don't move, all right? We're gonna turn on the lights now. You're gonna look beautiful. We wish everyone a Merry Christmas."

"Yeah, everyone a Merry Christmas," Ray repeated.

Jocelyn walked around the tree a second time and then spoke in a quiet voice. "Larry, did I give you that cord?"

From the outer extremity of the decorated tree came a bare hand with the light cord that Jocelyn had stripped and rolled into a copper ball. Jocelyn was now triumphant. "Now stand still," she ordered, "and we'll plug you in!" Jocelyn bent down to the wall outlet and tried to insert the mass of wire into the socket. It didn't fit. She reclaimed her kitchen knife from a coat pocket and shaped the raw wire into an arrow. "There, that should do it," she proudly announced.

"What the hell's going on here?" John Henry Butler's voice boomed. He was standing in the doorway,

his feet wide apart, his hair slicked back in a D.A. His
head nervously twisted side to side before he spoke
again. "You're going to electrocute that man. You know
you have him wired. He could fry!" In a rage, Butler
rushed forward and with both hands pushed the Christmas tree across the room. Larry fell backward and tumbled over, entangled in a net of lights and tinsel. Jocelyn
dashed to pick up the pieces. She stuffed wire and paper
into her pockets and, at the same time, helped Larry to
his feet.

Butler turned his attention to Ray. "I leave you five
minutes, man, and look at this mess! You can't stick live
wire into a socket! Jesus Christ, what would you do
if—?" Butler pulled Ray to the side of the bed and asked
in an anxious voice, "Do you know what time it is? I told
you I'd pick you up, you're supposed to be ready! I've got
that surprise I was tellin' you about, right outside. And
we got this date, remember, to do some shopping and
then get out of this crazy place!"

At first, Butler didn't notice that his enthusiasm
wasn't shared. He rattled on. "No more doin' jobs for
that lady downstairs with her candy boxes, she wouldn't
give you any of her candy if you asked for it, anyway."
Finally, Butler realized that at this moment Ray didn't
share his dream. "Look, man, I don't care what's going
on right now with you, we're gonna get out of here. This
is our chance, and you're not gonna blow it for me!"
Butler pushed Ray over to his drawer and pointed. "Get
your stuff together, and we're gettin' out of here. Cha,
cha, cha, Mexico, baby!"

Ray slowly opened his top drawer. "Take it, go
ahead, take everything you want," Butler urged. Ray
closed the drawer, opened it, and closed it again. "What's
wrong now?" Ray walked over to the Rogers and stood
sadly next to them. "Okay. Damn it, we'll take them. Is
that what you want? We'll take your friends here with us.
You, Christmas tree, you want to go with Ray here and
me? We're gonna go Christmas shopping, then take this
here vacation!"

Butler thought for a second. Then, as inevitable as a

diver in midair, he plunged on. "Well, why not? You two know what's happening. So what the hell?" Butler repeated his offer, this time with the confidence that something sounds better the second time.

"You guys need a guardian. You know I'm Ray's legal guardian. We're celebrating today 'cause I bought this new trailer outside, and I promised Ray I'd take him Christmas shopping and then we'd take off for Mexico. I mean, if I can be one guardian, what's two more? Look, if you have any property or inheritance like Ray, well, I can be like your manager. You know, take you places, do things for you? Things we can't do in this hole of a place."

Both Ray and Larry were rocking back and forth, shifting their balance from leg to leg. Jocelyn was quietly fussing over the broken bulbs and paper. "So come on," Butler said. "What do I have to say to you? We gotta leave right now while Mrs. Burr's at the welfare department. She thinks the monthly checks are late, but I've got them here in my wallet. So what do you say? Come on. You ever been Christmas shopping with money in your pocket?"

Jocelyn finished jamming things into her pockets, and turning to Butler, she asked, "Will you let us buy something?"

"Anything you want!" Butler was elated. He tapped the side of his leg and sweetened the pot. "We'll all go see Santa Claus and buy out the store, anything you want." Jocelyn's excitement spread to Larry and Ray. Bouncing into each other, they began to free Larry from his decorations.

It took half an hour to load the trailer with what Butler called "anything you want to show Santa Claus and take with you on a trip." John Henry Butler took one duffel bag and a sleeping bag. The Rogers loaded three suitcases, a toaster, one umbrella, and a cardboard box of pots and pans. Ray took one thing—his top drawer. Then raced back into the building and got his electric guitar. Ray bumped his head jumping into the front seat of the pickup.

God Rest Ye Merry Gentlemen

A wild woman and her trail of children came storming at the four travelers as they entered the Emporium. They collided inside the space between the sliding doors. The woman raved and stamped her feet. "Don't go in there—that Santa Claus is a complete imbecile—throwing candy to the children." She spun around and grabbed the innocent-looking Butler. "He says he's a psych major at State, can you believe that he was?"

"Who," asked a surprised Butler.

"Santa Claus," the woman continued. "He was throwing candy to the children so they'd pick it up and get the sticky stuff all over their new clothes, look at them! On those beautiful white Christmas dresses! I could kill him!" Before Butler or anyone could answer, the woman was pushing her children through the door, still complaining to anyone who would listen. "Big-deal psych major playing Santa Claus says the children will pick up the candy and it will abate their fear—can you imagine?—throwing candy at children in their new clothes? Who wants a picture of your kid with a faceful of candy, and look at their pretty clothes, just look . . ."

Butler should have taken this mania as a signal—a warning. Don't enter! Danger! One More Shopping Day Before Christmas.

The Emporium was packed. The air smelled of after-shave lotion and rubber. A mingling, moving mass of people jerked in spasms to the clatter of toy machine-gun fire and the whistle of an electric train. Orders were shouted, items held aloft like desperate offerings in the closing seconds of a stock exchange. Christmas decorations sagged, drooped, and fell into the throng. The iron grip between parent and child was broken. Panic was a breath away.

John Henry Butler's first outing with Ray and the Rogers wasn't going quite the way he had imagined. Mrs. Rogers thought she was hearing things. Raymond was afraid to move, then afraid to stop. Mr. Rogers had to go to the bathroom. Butler was finding out about parenthood.

"It's taped music! They're not hiding in the ceiling. It's Lawrence Welk, don't you— Excuse me— Look out! Sorry— Please stick with me That's right, I want you to— Don't touch that— Where's Ray? It's a mannequin— Where's Ray? No, it's not alive— No, not dead— Can you see him? Ray, over here— Where did you get that? No, there's no choir up on the roof— Hold hands— I said hold hands— I don't know where the toilet is— Is that where he went? Yes, we're going to see Santa Claus— He's over here someplace— We'll wait right here for Mr. Rogers— Oh, shit— Where's Jocelyn? That's right, let her find us— If we get lost, Ray, if we get separated, I'll meet you right here—no, we're all going to the bathroom—you got to—go ahead— Hey, no, we're all going to the bathroom together—Jocelyn will find us—"

After a millennium of shopping, Butler and his cohorts were standing safely in line to see Santa Claus. Only Jocelyn was missing. But Butler wasn't taking any chances. He had Raymond and Larry Rogers holding onto the picket fence that led to Santa's Workshops. As the three of them inched forward, Butler scanned the press of shoppers. "Maybe she'll just walk past—I want you guys to keep looking, but don't walk away, just keep looking, she's here someplace."

When Butler saw the commotion out of the corner of his eye, he knew it was trouble. Call it parent's intuition. "Come on, guys!" He pulled Ray and Mr. Rogers out of line and into the flood of bodies. Clothes were sailing into the air like scarves out of a magician's hat. Clothes that looked familiar. They floated in slow motion, an armless sweater. A dress without legs. And there were screams, mostly from women. And those bells that call the floor manager were ringing like fire alarms.

A tall man in a dark blue suit with holly in his button hole wrenched past Butler. Butler, Ray, and Mr. Rogers followed the blue streak. They wedged into the crowd that had formed a neat circle around . . . Butler couldn't believe his eyes. Screaming had turned to gasps. And women were trying to escape with their children. Butler closed his eyes. Then opened them.

Mrs. Rogers had undressed down to her underpants. Nope, now she was totally naked. Her pants were flying into the air. The man in the blue suit put out his arms as though he were going to stop an onrushing train. The train he was worried about was stripping a mannequin of velvet finery. Now there were two naked ladies in the central aisle of the Emporium. One had a plastic smile that didn't fit her contorted torso. The other, Mrs. Rogers, had the delighted smile of a woman about to try on a new evening gown.

The man with the holly boutonniere shouted, "Stop, put that dress back!" Mrs. Rogers paused and began to pull the gown back over her head. "No, no, stop, put it back on!" Mrs. Rogers let the new dress fall about her. She pleated it with her hands, pleased with its look and feel. The button man regained his speech. "That's a Dior evening dress." The appreciative spectators applauded both the manager's brilliance and Mrs. Rogers' modeling.

Butler pretended not to recognize the centerpiece of this drama. Mrs. Rogers paraded and kicked up the edge of the dress.

"Don't do that," Mr. Emporium warned. "Do you know this lady, does anyone, who are you and who sent you—is this some kind of stunt?" Mrs. Rogers didn't hear him. She was gathering up her underwear and stockings and thanking the other shoppers for helping her find her shoes. Now her arms were full, and she was eying another stunningly clothed mannequin. "No, you don't!" the protector of civility yelled as he clutched this still-clothed display. "Please, if anyone knows this lady, please help her to my office on the mezzanine." He held the smiling doll with one arm and pointed with the other.

Butler stepped forward. He knew a lot about managers and meetings in their offices. And he was quick when it came to surviving. Without missing a beat, he reached out and took Jocelyn's hand. Then he turned and whispered to the sweating manager, "Thank God you found her, she's been missing from the hospital for three days, we'd better get her back, um we'll send you the dress." The manager jerked his head at the thought. John Henry sealed the deal. "Or I can have her take off the dress right here—what do you want me to do?"

The manager forced a smile. It cracked like an opening fault line across his face. Barely able to speak, he concurred. "Send the dress back immediately." The drama at an end, the store quickly returned to its mad rush. Mrs. Rogers and her entourage retreated. She was now wearing a dark blue strapless evening gown with pearl sequin bodice and one tennis shoe. She still didn't understand the voices coming from above. Especially out in the parking lot. She asked about them, but Butler was too busy asking Ray about where he had gotten his new baseball hat. "You gave all your money to some kid standing next to the hats, I can't believe this, all of it . . ." Getting into the truck, Ray bumped his head again and again said he was sorry.

As the pickup and its yellow trailer pulled out of the brightly lit lot, Ray was tightly holding his new hat. Mrs. Rogers was leaning out the window studying the candescent heaven and that glorious music from invisible speakers.

> *God rest ye Merry Gentlemen,*
> *Let nothing you dismay.*
> *Remember Christ our Savior,*
> *Was born on Christmas Day,*
> *To save us all from Satan's power*
> *When we were gone astray . . .*

Just Follow The White Line

December 27, 1971

"You can't be lost, just follow the white line!" Mrs. Rogers said.

John Henry Butler shook his sleepy head but didn't answer. He wanted to complain, "How come one of you guys can't drive, why am I doin' all the drivin', three days three nights?" He held his tongue.

In Bakersfield, Mr. Rogers had taken a turn at driving. Actually, it was Mrs. Rogers' suggestion— "Sure Mr. Rogers can drive, he can drive anything." Mr. Rogers dropped the pickup into low and popped the clutch.

Then floored it! The pickup jumped like a jackrabbit down the road. Hop, hop, hop.

Yeah, thought Butler, good thing I could grab the wheel and turn off the ignition. Some driver. Some help. These guys need me more than children need parents.

Still, John Henry was enjoying his newfound responsibility. After all, he was a guardian, and this was his first full-time job. And it all might work out real well. They were already across the border without any trouble. All the way down, Butler feared the border—thought there would be a cuff man waiting for them. At the border check, they waved him through with his promise that "his parents" and "brother" were just visiting Mexico and would be returning to the States in a week.

Yeah, things were working real well. He had covered his trail by setting up a mail drop—an address he could use to funnel ATD checks to Mexico. The DPSS would simply send checks to this San Francisco mail service without any questions. And then, when he needed more money, he would contact this service and have them forward the checks to his Mexico location. Now all he had to do was find a good place for all of them to stay. And it would be high living. He had two thousand in cash, the trailer, and maybe, just maybe, well, the Rogers, like Raymond, might inherit some money or die and leave him their valuables. It was all working out, sorta. I mean he hadn't thought about taking the Rogers; they just came along with Ray. And what the hell, he couldn't help giggling over the image of Mrs. Burr discovering that Raymond was missing . . . and then the Rogers and her toaster, umbrella, and pans—all missing! He had this picture of her looking all over the house for her pots and pans!

The thing that surprised Butler was that he was getting to like Raymond and the Rogers. He liked the way the three of them cared for each other, and for him. I mean they were always trying to hug him; and it wasn't just that but the way they needed him. Need. That was it. Butler had never been needed. Or wanted. Or liked for being himself. Doing the best he could without pretending to be a tough shit. These new companions of his were different from anyone he had ever known. They weren't trying to "take him" or "beat him." They simply liked him. And he was beginning to like them.

They don't hate or fight! Everybody else seemed to be angry at something and just kinda blowin' it, getting in trouble, hitting something, no reasons, really, just getting pissed off and hurting themselves and anyone around them. Maybe it was because they had nothing to do, weren't as lucky as he was with these three. Being a guardian and all. Or maybe everyone was just crazy sick with having to beat up the next guy before he beats on you. Anyway, this Raymond and the Rogers were special—they didn't hate.

It would have been easy just to dump the three of them in Bakersfield. That's where this labor boss comes up and asks if the three sitting on the trailer step are for sale, for work, *braceros*. Offered Butler thirty-five dollars for the young man and twenty dollars for the older pair. He told the fat slob to kiss off. The fat man with the giant belt buckle just laughed.

What did he know, Butler thought. So they look funny in old clothes and an evening dress. And they can't drive a car. They can like you, and that's a first. In fact, everything seems a first for them. I mean I got to teach them about driving. All the way from Los Angeles to the border, I had the three of them holding imaginary steering wheels and making motor noises by buzzing their lips. Hell, they loved it. What a gas! Laughed so much. Ray was bouncing up and down on the seat, humming and driving, turning that imaginary wheel, braking for emergencies!

Ray loved the feeling of being in the pickup truck. Flying down the road. Things moved so quickly. He tried to watch a road sign and tell the meaning, but the sign jerked past his head and was running behind the truck before he could tell what it was trying to say. A cold river of air made his feet ache. And a stream of air slipped past the window opening, making a hissing sound. The last light of day was walking across the dusty windshield in puffs of orange and pink. There was this neon tug-of-war. First the sky with its brilliance. Then the dashboard with its fluorescent lines and numbers. A final burst of color streaked across the window, followed by shades of blue changing to purple and then darkness. It was like a blanket being pulled over the truck. In this soft darkness, the lights inside the truck became glowing eyes.

Ray felt wonderful. He got to sit next to the window. And there next to him were his friends. Friends were not new to Ray, but these friends traveling in the truck with him were somehow different. Friends for Ray had been mostly things and places. Things like his WHIZ guitar and the objects in his top bureau drawer. Places like the bench in Golden Gate Park. Or people like Letty on Haight Street and Jake at the carousel. Ray visited these friends regularly. He went to them. But these friends in the truck came to him. Asked if they could help put up his Christmas lights. Taught him how to drive. Let him keep his baseball hat. Butler was going to show him how to pitch a baseball and let him wash the trailer and pickup—by himself.

Ray rocked back and forth in the moving truck. The springs in the seat sneezed with each shift of weight. Ray was crying, and he didn't know why. He was happy, and he was crying. He held his hands over his eyes so the others wouldn't think he was sad or hurt.

"What happened to the lines?" Mrs. Rogers' hope of following the center line was gone. Without warning, the pickup and trailer were bouncing down a washboard road. Rock and gravel kicked at the underside of the fen-

ders. Dust crawled into the cab of the truck and mingled
with the smell of an overheated engine. Butler sat upright. Tense and nervous. Both his hands gripped the
wobbling steering wheel. Mr. Rogers woke from his day-
long nap and asked, "Where are we, did we pass Dis-
neyland?" No one could answer. Mrs. Rogers wriggled,
then straightened out her evening gown. Finally, she
gleaned some revelation from the headlights of the
pickup.

"We're almost there!" Butler grimaced. Then
snapped, "We better be someplace soon, 'cause we've
been out of gas for about the last ten miles."

Mrs. Rogers was the first to sight land. "There,
straight ahead." Butler let out a deep sigh. Mr. Rogers'
slumbering head returned to its place against Ray's
shoulder. Ray uncrossed his fingers.

Butler guided the gasping pickup and its trailer to a
quiet corner of the sleeping town. He parked in the only
bare space he could find. It looked like a field between a
row of buildings and shacks with corrugated roofs. The
engine heaved as tappets continued their metal count-
down. Then it was quiet. Stillness wrapped around the
four travelers like a welcome blanket. Their bodies relaxed, escaped to the stars.

When Butler awoke in the morning, he was surrounded by sound and color. Conversations swarmed like
bees around the trailer. Butler looked outside. Melons
passed hand to hand past the trailer porthole. Balloons
dangled in the air. Scarlet gladiolas and yellow dahlias
poured over their basket containers. Fruit stood in
golden pyramids. A brush-and-pail merchant passed the
trailer. His mountain of brooms and clanking buckets totally obscured him. The moving pile of bristles and metal
pails had the look of a gigantic armadillo. Children
skipped past this great beast with Mickey Mouse masks
tied to the tops of their heads, crowding toward a puppet show.

Blankets snapped in the air. Tortillas steamed on
kerosene stoves, then were stacked like records. Tea,

soda pop, and hardware vendors engaged in animated bartering with patient customers. A pig on a string paraded to the courtship of a new owner. Butler woke his fellow travelers. "Jesus Christ, we're sitting right in the middle of a flea market!"

Ray joined Butler at his porthole view of the world. He looked out and smiled as if it were a dream come true. All the men looked like Elvis Presley.

The Rogers were electrified. Thrilled by the giving and taking. Buying and selling. Mrs. Rogers was first to leave the musty trailer. She jumped out the side door in hot pursuit of a good deal. With her toaster tucked under her arm, she waded into the sea of white-clad shoppers. Butler had trouble closing the door behind her. Everyone had something to sell or trade or just talk about. Words flew like butterflies, and Butler didn't have a net.

By midmorning John Henry Butler was drunk—and had a problem. Actually, three problems. Mrs. Rogers had traded her toaster for three chickens. And they were jumping around the inside of the trailer in aborted efforts to peck their way to freedom. Mrs. Rogers was chasing them, trying to feed them a handful of Cheerios. Mr. Rogers and Raymond were afraid of the red-eyed birds. So they had climbed into the cab of the pickup. "What in hell are we going to do with three," Butler hollered. "Did you say three of those—Jesus Christ, I turn my back for ten seconds, three of them, turn around, and first I catch you about to sell the carburator, you can't just, you have three of them, three . . ."

After hours of directions and lines drawn in the dust and four gallon cans of gasoline and two more beers, Butler and his gang were ready to leave. Mrs. Rogers wouldn't part with her chickens, so a tarp was stretched across the back of the truck. "The chickens can ride in the back of the truck, but no, not in the trailer."

Several miles away, the dirt road intersected a paved highway. Once again, there were lines to follow. When Mrs. Rogers inspected her "lovely chickens," she uncovered a terrible sight. The chickens had bashed around in back of the truck, crashing against the metal bed until they were a bloody pulp. It was hot and dusty, and flies were already attacking the gorged bodies when Butler ripped open the tarp, grabbed the dying and dead birds, and swung them into the air.

They Would Probably Rather Be Dead

January 20, 1972

Sherry Croce and J. B. Carver met for their regular lunch at Bill's Place on Clement Street. Bill seated them personally at "their table" next to the sliding-glass door that led to the outdoor garden. It was exactly ten minutes to noon, a little ahead of the rush. Bill's Place was a favorite for social-service workers in San Francisco. Bill had retired from social service so he could, as he called it, "let his hair down."

Croce and Carver loved coming to Bill's. It was always busy with the coming and going of onetime clients. And there was the atmosphere. No other hamburger restaurant had his Marie Antoinette crystal chandeliers, Japanese garden complete with a goldfish pond and miniature wooden bridge, and ancient, white-haired waitresses. Best of all, Bill didn't mind if the lunch crowd supplemented his menu of burgers and shakes with a few carrots of their own.

Carver plopped into his chair and immediately opened up a *Time* magazine. Sherry bit her lip. Once again, there was this unspoken feeling that everything was going wrong. That they could no longer control their work or their lives. The same problems kept repeating over and over. Nothing was getting better.

Sherry sat with one foot crooked underneath her and waited patiently for Carver to say something. The menus had come and gone before Carver looked up from his magazine. "See this?" Jim tapped his magazine. "Sixty-three percent of the readers think handicapped people should be kept out of sight."

Miss Croce tried a joke. "They are out of sight, they're missing completely."

"They would probably rather be dead!" Jim continued to read from his magazine. "That's what most people think."

Miss Croce carefully unwrapped her sliced carrots and glanced over at Carver's noodle salad and candy bar from the department's vending machine. They both ordered a Bill's Burger and strawberry shakes. After a while, Jim curled the magazine and stuffed it into his lunch bag.

"You know," he said without looking at Sherry, "they are going to hire eleven more city attorneys to handle crime in the streets." His statement didn't draw a response. There were so many things now that they couldn't talk about.

Sherry dragged a paper napkin from the chrome dispenser. "Did you know Ray Martinez is missing?" she asked. "Has been for a week, and Mrs. Burr won't tell me where he is, says his aunt takes him on unexpected vacations and she can't control that old lady . . ."

Sherry methodically folded the napkin into a small rectangle. Then pulled out another and repeated the process. The napkins looked like tiny white surrender flags. "Um," Carver said, "I haven't had much time to poke around on the Martinez case, but he's not with his aunt."

Sherry placed both hands over the tiny pile of napkins and asked, "Oh, what have you—?"

"I visited his church and found some addresses," Carver continued. "His aunt, she's living up in Concord. She's eighty years old and doesn't get around much anymore. And she hasn't talked with Ray in over six months."

"That's interesting," Sherry said, opening her clutch purse and withdrawing a note pad and pen. "Give me her name and number."

Carver reached into a coat pocket, then a shirt pocket; finally, he dug one hand into his pants pocket and retrieved a stash of papers. "It's here someplace. Yeah, sure, here it is." Carver smiled triumphantly and pushed the card of a local realtor across the table.

"You buying or selling?" Sherry was quick to observe.

"No, no, on the back, look on the back," Carver reported. "It's the address you want."

Sherry slipped the card into an empty fold in her wallet. Then quickly returned her attention to the pile of paper in front of Carver. "Your notes?" she asked with a grin.

"Yeah, yeah, my notes and a parking ticket." The parking ticket angered Carver. With one hand, he ironed out the ticket against the table. "There should be a law against parking meters. No one ever voted yes on parking meters—now that's a case those fancy new attorneys will never bring."

"Here, eat a carrot," Sherry said, offering consolation. "It's better for you than that plastic-wrapped—what do you call that?"

"Mrs. Hubbard's Home Cooked," Carver said with confidence, showing Sherry the package. "Look here, it says: 'Compliments of Bill's Burger. Prepared daily in our kitchens for James B. Carver, supervisor of Fraud Unit 210.'"

"Nice." Sherry chuckled and with a sweep of her

hand removed the pile of napkins by sliding them into her purse. "Speaking of fraud," she asked briskly, "did you ever find my file boxes?"

"Yep, they're at Bekins Storage—lost like everyone else's!"

"Great, just great." Sherry tilted her carrot in pessimistic salute.

"I do my best, ma'am," drawled Carver's John Wayne imitation. "And I found out something about Ray Martinez."

Sherry placed her elbows on the table and dropped her head into the fold of both hands. She was conscious of her long fingers and manicured nails. A warm blush in her cheeks. She wondered if the top button on her blouse was buttoned. Hoped it wasn't. Leaning across the table, she wanted to say something warm, something sexy. "So tell me," Sherry asked in a soft voice. "Tell me," she repeated. Then held her breath. She reached to see if her blouse was buttoned. Her hand stayed at her throat as she pulled back and sat upright. "Where, where is my client?"

"I don't know," came a reply. "I found out this Raymond Martinez—do you know his father was fifty-five when Ray was born and his mother was sixteen? She died when he was nine. The aunt says Ray was jet black at birth and could fit in a shoe box. Poor kid had some bad breaks when—has this Raymond of yours ever been travel trained?"

Sherry's head reeled back, and her hand crashed to the table. "You know what happened when we tried to travel train? All the hassle with Muni not wanting responsibility and the supervisors alarmed about putting undesirables on public transit." Sherry's voice increased in loudness and pitch. Then calmed. "So we get our test case, you remember Philip?"

J. B. Carver nodded.

"Sweet Philip, Philip Alexander. Everyone called him Jolly Green Giant because he always wore that green suit with a bow tie and was so tall. For weeks I stood with him at the bus stop trying to teach him, you know, to get on the right bus . . ."

"That was just one of those cases," Carver offered.

"You know how I finally got him to recognize the right bus—it was slips of paper with the number eighteen, I pinned them into the lining of his green jacket, knew he wouldn't go out without it. Everything is perfect, we've got the best, the kindest person imaginable for our test. If it works for Philip, we have hundreds waiting to get out and learn to move around the city to shelter workshops, museums, oh, Jesus."

"I remember, Sherry, you don't have to—" Carver murmured. He stretched both his hands toward her and gently tried to quiet Sherry's pain.

Sherry's eyes flooded with tears. She didn't know if she was crying for Philip or for herself. Her voice broke into sobs. "Finally, the day comes, and our sweet Philip has his green suit and he's all scared and happy about going solo. All by himself across town. That's all we wanted, just a bus ride.

"It was my fault. Why didn't I think of it? I should have known what might happen, oh, I should have—the bus wasn't that crowded, but I should have known. When Philip tries to be friends with a little girl riding on the bus the mother of the child panics and has Philip arrested. By the time I find out what's happened and get to the jail it's too late. Oh, Jesus! Philip just looked at me with those big innocent eyes. His head was shaved, and they took his suit; and, and, he was raped. Repeatedly raped by other inmates because he was in for child molesting. All he wanted was to be friends. They wouldn't even give him his suit, his suit back." Miss Croce wiped the table with her bare hand. Wiped it again and again.

Carver understood this. She tried so desperately to give order to a world of chaos and desperation. He knew that her work was the one thing she understood and the one thing that gave her life meaning. She had work to do. They both had work to do. That's what mattered—the job—doing it right. And as long as they had work to do, they would be together. J. B. Carver spoke matter-of-factly—like a professional talking to a professional. It was their way. Their fate. "I've got some more news for you about your Raymond Martinez. Some other things you should know."

Sherry listened intently.

Carver continued. "Your John Henry Butler, Ray's court-appointed guardian and Mrs. Burr's stepson, well, he just got out of the state penitentiary—nothing big, but I wouldn't want to walk around the block with him."

If You Can't Be Out You Must Be Safe

January 30, 1972
Trailer Park Tingubatu
Sixty Miles South of Uruapan, Mexico

"You're out!" Butler yelled. "Look, put your thumb in the air like this and shout with me, 'You're out!'" John Henry Butler was coaching the concept of "out" for the eighty-third time. His team—which is to say, the Rogers and Ray Martinez—was having trouble with that.

Butler tried once again. He pitched the ball to Ray. Ray swung and sent the beach ball they were using toward the trailer-park ash cans. After stumbling around for a minute, Butler picked up the ball and raced toward the yellow trailer. All the way he kept screaming at Ray, "Keep going, you're going to first base, that's it, keep going!" It's hard to run and laugh. A few steps from the trailer Ray wheeled around and embraced the charging Butler. "Oh, no!" Butler moaned. "You're supposed to keep running, get to the base, don't let me touch you with the ball or else—you're out. Look now I've got to tag you and— You're out!" Butler repeated the play as if on instant replay— "You're out!" Butler raised his arm in a great sweep, and with his thumb orbiting the air, he yelled, "You're out!"

Ray just stood there smiling. Butler tried again. "Look! My thumb's in the air. That means . . . Oh, forget it, next batter, come on Jocelyn, it's your turn. Ray you can't stand there, you're out."

Butler studied the new batter. Then looked over his shoulder like all good pitchers. And noticed Raymond with one hand on the yellow trailer. "Ray, you're out. Once you're out, you can't go to the base."

"But he's on base and you said once someone reached base you can't be out." Mrs. Rogers added her two cents.

Butler mumbled to himself, "I don't think Casey Stengel has this problem." He walked over to Ray and took his hand, then explained once again the rules of the diamond. "Okay Ray, let's try again. You hit the ball and run to first base, then to the red ash can—that's second base, then to Larry's coat, then back to home. And you don't let me tag you, or else you're out."

Once more, Butler went into his Juan Marichal delivery. Once again, Ray Martinez lifted a clean base hit. "Good hit," Butler yelled, and started off after the fleeing beach ball. When Butler turned around, Ray was streaking right past the pitching mound and heading into second base. Butler gave frantic chase. "No, not that base, you've got to go to first base first, then second!" Ray wouldn't take his hand off the ash-can base.

"All right," Butler ordered. "Everyone over here."

The team circled their coach. "I want to talk to you guys about what it means to be safe, 'cause you see, you guys don't understand what it means to be out!"

A tall, blonde, wispy-haired woman approached the confab at second base. She stood off to the side as Butler defined "out."

"You can't have a game without out . . . that's what makes the game work." The wispy woman, whose name was Star Flower, listened politely until he finished the lecture. "Mind if we play?" she asked.

Butler didn't like the hippies in the trailer park. Didn't understand what they were doing in Mexico. Why they were against the war in Vietnam and wore their hair long. And why they would take the wheels off their vans and buses. Why in the world would they do that? He had kept a distance. Parked the yellow trailer next to the Mexican families staying in the park. The woman asked again, "Can we play with you, you know the children would really like to play." The children weren't wearing clothes—a sight that confused Butler. In his mind, people were supposed to wear clothes—especially Americans.

Though Butler's mind froze, he agreed. It was hard to say no to a bunch of kids jumping around. So he agreed. "It's okay with me, but I want those kids to be wearin' clothes, I mean if we're going to play baseball."

The woman told the children to get on "uniforms" so they could play. Children scampered away and returned wearing an odd assortment of capes, feathers, and little league batting helmets. Butler shook his head. The woman had one more request. "Mind if my old man over there, his name is Pipes, mind if he does the 'play by play' announcing? He idolizes Vince Scully and it would be real important for him if he could call a game." Butler nodded. The situation was out of his control, and he knew it.

"Everybody stand for the national anthem," Pipes announced. Butler and his team—Mrs. Rogers at short-stop, Mr. Rogers on first, and Ray playing the field—stood at attention. Across from them stood their opponents, five hippie children and three hippie adults.

Everyone was swiveling his head, looking for a flag, when Star Flower called out, "Don't worry, the flag is in your mind." Raymond took off his baseball cap during the singing and tried to find a picture of a flag some-where in his mind.

The game turned out to be pure hysterical mayhem. The hippies led off the top of the first with "seeing-eye singles," bloopers, a double steal, four home runs, one hit batter, and a perfectly executed "suicide squeeze." With each hit or run, Butler raced about trying to tell Jocelyn where to throw the ball and Mr. Rogers where to keep his foot. "You have to step on the base to make an out!"

Pipes was preaching the inner meaning of each play to a growing cluster of hippies and Mexicans. Their cheering and chanting got to Butler. He didn't like losing or being made fun of. Frustrated with his teammates, he made an unassisted triple play. Actually caught a pop fly and raced around the bases tagging out runners that had taken off for home . . . or just taken off. Pipes—not only the official announcer but the official scorekeeper, too—credited Butler with a spectacular play. "Ladies and gen-tlemen, you have just witnessed baseball history—an unassisted four outs!"

Butler kept trying to play his game while everyone else played theirs. It took him a long time to realize that everyone else was more fascinated by playing than win-ning. They happily let Jocelyn circle the bases in re-verse. And helped Ray when he stumbled between bases. Mr. Rogers was a problem base runner. He liked to stand still. One of the hippie kids ran for him. Butler cleared the bases with a blast over the green trailer. The fans cheered, drank lots of beer, then joined the game.

After a while, you couldn't tell who was on whose team, what the score was, and why Jocelyn was leading football yells.

In his postgame interview, Pipes took his broom-handle microphone and started walking around the field. "Well, fans, this has been quite a game, the players are all to be congratulated, of course ABC is delighted to have brought you this game and a word with today's players—wait, wait, we have one of the star players right here. . . ."

Pipes put his arm around a smiling Ray Martinez and, posturing like a television interviewer, asked Ray to "step a little closer, that's it, now tell the folks watching this game at home um, just how did it feel out there today playing both shortstop and center field?" Ray just grinned and shook both shoulders up and down. Pipes continued his patter. "Well, I know you must be anxious to get to the showers, just one more question." Pipes took the broom from in front of his face and waved it in front of Ray— "Tell me, how many years have you been playing in the big leagues?"

Ray answered confidently, "Six hundred and forty-six home runs."

Without pause, Pipes asked, "And would you like to say hello to anyone special, maybe one of those little leaguers watching this game of the week?"

Ray grabbed the handle microphone. "I want to say hello to all my friends, Mrs. Burr and Jake and Letty, she's a friend of mine. . . ." As Pipes moved on, Ray received the customary slapping of hands from the other players.

Pipes was now talking to the afternoon sky, or at least that's the way it looked. "Before I pass it back to you guys in the booth, let me, yes I've got him right here, let me ask a few questions to this year's manager of the year." Pipes reached out and pulled Butler's shoulder from behind. Butler spun around with a look that could kill! "Wow, slow down, baby," Pipes cautioned. "That was really some great game you and your team there played today. Can you tell us where you are from?"

Butler pushed the microphone away. Pipes persisted, he knew the secret of getting through a tight situation was to just keep talking, say anything. "So, so, where did you find that tall guy, he's got great movement and yeah, that lady does a lot of picking up, never saw a player clean the field while the game was, no, no insult, you got a good group of people there . . ."

The flood of questions finally worked. Butler took the broom handle and asked a question of his own. "Say, why did you take the wheels off your vans, that's real stupid!"

Star Flower glided between the two men. "It's the native way—the Aztecs let their children have wheeled toys, but it was against Aztec law for adults to use a wheel." Star Flower painted the sky with her hands. "They were content in this place, didn't want anything else or anything more, and this was their way of telling the gods that they would not be leaving."

"Oh," grunted Butler, confused. Then looked up into the hills and at the circle of wheelless vans and buses before offering a final "Bullshit."

Pipes handed Butler a beer and started humming, "If you've got time, we've got the beer—Milllleeerrrs Beeer hmm hm . . ." In appreciation, Butler drained the beer in one tilt of his head, then crushed the empty can and tossed it toward the hippie encampment.

John Henry Butler was mystified. Everything had turned upside down. The hippies he didn't like had turned out to be all right. They gave him some beer, and it was fun playing baseball with them. But they didn't laugh at him when he told them he was taking care of the Rogers and Raymond. Instead, Star Flower walked up to Butler and told him he was like the God Quetzalcoatl— "a blond man like you that gave the Indians the gift of corn. A god that took care of people like you are doing. Do you know he predicted he would return in the calendar cycle of the year 1520? That's the year Cortés came." John Henry enjoyed watching Star Flower and hearing her talk. "When Cortés invaded this land, the Indians believed that if you killed an enemy in battle, your soul wouldn't go to heaven. They couldn't understand the Spanish killing and wounding during a battle."

"Yeah, that's amazing," Butler agreed.

Star Flower welcomed a possible convert. "You know the Aztec priests could never wash or cut their hair. And they were the only ones allowed to wear feathers and bright-colored clothing. That's why the Indians like us. We don't like war that kills; and look at us, we love colorful clothing. Of course, all the Aztec priests were gay but, well you can see we're not gay, not all of us. What do you think, do you want to join our circle? It's all right, I've talked with Pipes and the others."

Butler gazed at the graveyard of old buses and the eyes of Star Flower. He was confused by it all. Everything was happening so quickly. He didn't answer. "That's all right," Star Flower said quietly. "Let the moon affect your thoughts—we're all Mexicans here— children from the navel of the moon."

Children From The Navel Of The Moon

February 19, 1972

Star Flower tapped lightly on the door of the trailer. It was the twelfth cycle of the moon. Actually, it was late afternoon. A time for celebration and sacrifice. She stood there naked.

She was saying something, but John Henry Butler didn't hear what it was. Star Flower's nipples pointed like pink number-three erasers. And her tanned body shined with hot oil. The sun falling from its place in the sky branded his eyes with light. The brilliant globe sat on her shoulder and made bursts of blue dance across her body. John Henry Butler had to look away. Nakedness belongs in the dark. Something you buy or take. He didn't understand nakedness standing there in the daylight. So calm and beautiful.

Star Flower touched her lips with one finger. Then she spoke again. "We are having a celebration, at sundown," she said, "on the old pyramid, over there—" Star Flower pointed to a plateau behind the trailer park. At first, Butler thought the flat mountain was a volcano, but upon closer examination he realized that the slope of the hill was shaped like saw marks or teeth or giant steps of stone. Butler squinted at the pyramid glowing in the slanting light. He jammed both hands into his back pockets and made fists. His jeans tightened around his crotch. Star Flower continued. "We want to invite you and your friends to be our special guests." Then, as if reading the questions in Butler's eyes, she concluded, "We are the treasure, you know, and our feast is tonight

and you and your friends, we hope you will join us . . ."
John Henry turned and glanced first toward the trailer
and then at Star Flower. She turned and walked away.
Her body moving as gracefully as a desert mirage. John
Henry realized that she had the hots for him. That's it,
she likes me and wants to run away from Pipes and his
group of "far outs."

Butler called Ray and the Rogers and told them
they were going to a party.

He waited and waited. Star Flower's lovely, naked
body flashed like some "coming attraction" in his mind.
"Come on, come on you guys, let's go!" Mr. Rogers
couldn't find his teeth. Ray kept asking, "What are you
doing?" like a tape loop. And Mrs. Rogers was struggling
into her evening dress. "Come on, how long's it take,
Jesus, leave the teeth!" Butler paced back and forth in
front of the rocking trailer. Ray followed him step for
step, like a shadow. When Butler banged his hand
against the side of the trailer, Ray did likewise. Butler
swung around toward Ray. "What the hell are *you*
doing?" he yelled.

"What are you doing?" Ray repeated.

"If you ask me that," Butler snapped, then caught
himself— "I'm standing here waiting for the twinky
twins in there to get it together so we can get to this
party; and then I'm goin' to show you some timely
moves. Have you ever had a lady, you know, naked, making love?"

'Raymond rolled his head. "I don't know."

Butler smiled and clapped his hands. "Well, tonight, might just be, you keep an eye on me, on the
moves you know." Ray stepped closer. Butler backed up.
"Don't stay too close man, just keep the eyes goin' all
right, all right."

Pipes was bedecked in a feathery halo. Otherwise,
he, too, was without clothes—as were most of the twenty
young adults and children there. They made a human
circle at the base of the pyramid, and Pipes was in the
center. When the visitors approached the circle—in

evening dress, WHIZ guitar, and baseball cap—Star Flower detached herself from the group and gazed at her new disciples with glowing delight. Those wonderful flying erasers! They were too much for Butler. He covered an eye and then streaked his hands through his blond hair.

"I'm glad you could make it," Star Flower said with a soft pant in her voice. . . . "Pipes is about to start the ceremony, you know he taught anthropology at Berkeley before coming here."

Pipes took several deep breaths. His slow, rhythmic breathing brought calm and stillness to the gathering. Sitting cross-legged, Pipes ceremoniously opened a Pee Chee folder and began reading incantations scribbled on sheets of yellow binder paper.

One morning, the Sun shot an arrow from the sky. It landed on the house of mirrors, and from the opening which it made in the rock emerged a man and a woman. Both were incomplete. They had nothing below the thorax, and through the fields they would skip like sparrows. But merging in a profound kiss, they gave birth to a sun who became the origin of men.

Children ran in and about the circle like streamers of colored paper on a May pole. Their peals of laughter made more vivid the somber tones of Pipes and the occasional tinkling of tamborines. A cactus drink circulated in a plastic pitcher. And the air was sweet and heady. Dust floating skyward reflected a gold mist. Paper lanterns danced in the breeze. Heads nodded approval.

So has it been said by Tochihuitzin,
so has it been said by Coyolchiuhqui:
It is not true, it is not true
that we come to this earth to live.

We come only to sleep, only to dream.
Our body is a flower.
As grass becomes green in the springtime,
so our hearts will open and give forth buds,
and then they wither.
So did Tochihuitzin say.

Star Flower sat next to the yellow trailer people. "Isn't it wonderful?" she whispered to Raymond. "Pipes is reading from the original Aztec. The Aztec myth of creation and Deeds of Life. It's from the Codices." Butler was glad that Star Flower had turned to talk to Raymond. That way he could steal a glance at her splendid tits. They quivered with each breath. "The Codices were taken by the Spaniards, the two-thousand-year history of a people. Most of the library was destroyed, but what is left is in Spain and at U.C. Berkeley." Ray returned Star Flower's sincerity with a San Francisco Giants' statistic. Pipes continued setting words in the sky in place of the setting sun. The lanterns came alive with soft colored light.

The flowers sprout, they are fresh, they grow;
they open their blossoms,
and from within emerge the flowers of song;
among men You scatter them, You send them.
You are the singer!

Star Flower sat up on her knees. Butler inched forward and twisted so that he could see all of her. Accompanying Pipes, he chanted to himself praise of petals and seeds. And hearts on fire. Others were beginning to feel the spirit of the cactus drink and the rhythm of palms slapping bodies. A few in the circle began to dance in time with the words in the sun.

> One day we must go,
> one night we will descend into the region of mystery.
> Here, we only come to know ourselves;
> only in passing are we here on earth.
> In peace and pleasure let us spend our lives;
> come, let us enjoy ourselves.
> Let not the angry do so; the earth is vast indeed!
> Would that one lived forever;
> would that one were not to die!

Men and women were dancing. Their bodies coming together and pulling apart. Swirling like the whirlpool in your head when you're stoned or intoxicated. Chanting and clapping. Butler realized that everyone knew the words of Pipes's prayers. Even Ray seemed to know the words. He was surely repeating each stanza with conviction. And strumming on his cordless guitar. Mrs. Rogers was starting to take off her dress.

> Remove trouble from your hearts, oh my friends.
> As I know, so do others;
> only once do we live.
> Let us in peace and pleasure spend our lives;
> come, let us enjoy ourselves!
> Let not those who live in anger join us,
> the earth is so vast.
> Oh! that one could live forever!
> Oh! that one never had to die!

Ray was dancing and doing his Elvis Presley imitations in the midst of jutting arms and rolling hips. Mrs. Rogers bounced up and down, her evening dress wrapped around her body like a velvet belt. Her sagging torso, with its great quilt marks and white buttocks, stood out in the bronze blur of flesh around her. Star Flower tried to pull Butler's pants off, but he tugged and kept them on. He was too embarrassed to go naked or dance. He worried that his body would betray him. Would Star Flower's slightest gesture make his penis grow stiff? Frightened, he moved into the darkness of a wheelless bus and drank.

Next morning Butler awoke to Raymond's insistent questions. "What are you doing? What are you doing? What are you doing? What are you doing?" Butler's head was a drum. Ray pounded again. "What are you doing?" Butler staggered to his feet, and using Ray's WHIZ guitar as a cane, he and Ray limped back to their trailer. Their wheelless trailer. Now Mrs. Rogers was examining the black metal stumps that used to hold Goodyear rubber and grinning. Butler didn't, couldn't say a thing. "We sacrificed them!" she said.

A Lot Of Words In My Head

February 23, 1972

"It always rains at one o'clock. Why does it always rain and then stops just like that?" John Henry Butler was talking; but as usual no one else was listening. Things were not going so well.

In the rush to leave San Francisco, he'd forgotten to inform DPSS about a change of address for the Rogers. So their checks were still going to Mrs. Burr's. The old bitch must have been up there smiling her head off, he thought. I'm doing all the work, and she was getting all the money. I should have known that's the way things would work out. I'm always on the wrong end of a deal.

Always. Nothing I try works out. I mean the mail drop should've been a perfect screen. The DPSS would send checks to this Mexico address. How did those yoyos ever think of holding up Raymond's ATD check until they could do a personal interview. Now all they are sending are form letters about an interview. I'm Ray's *guardian*, not some toy on someone's string.

And the money. It goes so fast. Four days in a fancy beach-front hotel—with two luxury suites. That was another mistake. Two rooms. I should have kept the Rogers under lock and key. Shit, they used room service like it was a free lunch. And of course the hotel didn't tell me about it. Hell, they were laughing all the way to the bank. In just one day they spent $438 on meals, another $100 on telephone calls, and $86 in the Moonlight Boutique.

Then Mrs. Rogers purchased a bathing suit and robe to go with her evening dress. She was just a case. I mean you had to watch her all the time. And watch the tires on the pickup. The mental ropes that keep most people together just didn't exist for Mrs. Rogers. If she saw something she wanted, she chased it. Like her rock collection. Why in the world did she collect rocks? Not jade or glass or pretty rocks but just rocks. She had the largest rock collection in the world. It took up half the trailer. She was always so happy. Like Ray. Whew. It's hard to yell at a contented rock collector who's old enough to be your grandmother.

And Mr. Rogers wasn't any help. Jesus, he's such a telephone pole. I mean you know he's there, but he stands so still and quiet you forget him. You can't talk to him much. I mean he hardly even answers. Just agrees by shaking his head. I wish he'd get angry or shout or listen to that radio of his or do anything besides stand and watch Mrs. Rogers pick up rocks. I'm always bumping into him. Always the same look. The same clothes. The same smell.

Ray at least puts on a change of clothes every so often and tries to sing songs on that guitar of his. He also likes to be tickled. You know Mr. Rogers is the only person I've ever known that isn't ticklish. Jesus. You know I like Ray. He's got a lot of things about him, the way he tries. He can imitate anything. Course he can't remember it but he sure can repeat a movement or lyric. Sometimes I wish he'd learn something new. He's like a broken record. Like once he gets started he won't stop—like "What are you doing?" He must ask me that a hundred times a day. If I'm walking down to the trailer office he asks, "What are you doing?" If I'm taking a piss he comes up and asks me, "What are you doing?" All day long. It's drivin' me crazy. Then ten minutes later he's asking me again.

Early this morning I got fed up with him. "I won't speak to you 'til you use some new words," I told him. "Ask me another question, any other question!" You know what he said? "I got a lot of words in my head!" What kind of answer is that? God, how nice it would be to talk to someone besides myself! And nice if Ray wouldn't try to hug me every time he sees me.

"I got a lot of words in my head."

Exactly! Ray's mind is full of moving words. They float past his mind's eye like silken banners. Words so beautiful and illusive. Words so carefully caressed that so suddenly disappear. Then other words crowd into the stream. They also fade away. Nothing keeps words in place. The knot that for you and me binds words into meaning does not exist for Ray. The ability to build words into empires of thought does not exist. So images skitter past his struggling grasp. A musical score with no performance.

Like an infant, Ray does not know his left from his right. He has no mental map of his own shape and displacement. Thus, a picture of himself shows only a blob with two large eyes and an open mouth. Thus, Ray often knocks his head against the tops of doorways or slams into chairs and tables. He can not "learn" from the experience of knocking his head on the trailer. Each day he hits his head the same way. Each day the trailer doorway is a new strait to navigate with a vessel of unknown dimensions. Every day, everything is new.

Everything important in Ray's world must be painstakingly repeated, repeated, and repeated. If not, it's lost. All the while flashing, random impressions make constant assault against the ideas Ray is trying to repeat and hold onto.

Ray's only control besides repetition is the passionate pursuit of an idea, person, or thing that chances into his orbit. If Ray sees a friend, his friendship must be reconfirmed on the spot. To taste this friendship, Ray must embrace it, hold it, cause it to respond. For this moment like all others will quickly change. "Hold on don't let go!" There are few memories. No illusions. No explanations. Only moments. Each moment is a complete lifetime.

"I got a lot of words in my head!"

"Hey, why does it always rain at one o'clock?" Butler asked once again. Finding no answer, he began to unload the Rogers' clothing from the trailer. Once all the clothing was piled on the ground in sagging paper bags, Butler asked Jocelyn, "Do me a favor, I want to see how much clothing you can put on, yeah, kinda like a world record." Mrs. Rogers loved that idea! After twenty minutes of tucking, buttoning, giggling, wriggling, lacing, and stuffing, Mrs. Rogers looked like a clothes rack in a dormitory.

"Now show me," Butler said, satisfied with the layered look, "can you say, '*You're Out!*' That's it, one thumb in the air and swoop it around. Good! Good! All right, everyone in the truck. Come on. Put the extra clothes in here."

"What are you doing?" Ray asked.

Butler's ring raked against the knuckles of the steering wheel. And sweat crawled down his scalp, wetting and curling the ends of his hair. His tapping ring gave a rattling cadence to his thoughts. It was almost as if he were arguing to himself—repeating some secret he had discovered and rehearsed a thousand times. Larry sat crunched against Butler. As usual, he was petrified, arms stiff and pinched against his body, like a lightning rod waiting for heaven's blast. Jocelyn, squeezed like a laundry bag between Larry and Ray, was holding Ray's hand.

"It's all right to do what I've got to do," Butler said, more to himself than to the others, "'cause everybody gets something, and everybody's got to get something. Yeah, that's the way it works. . . ." Larry gave a fearful, wide-eyed glance toward Jocelyn, but she was confronting a problem of her own. She was being buried alive by her clothing. Sweaters, dresses, and coats so bunched up around her neck that her face was barely visible under the rising tide. These many layers of fabric were frictionless as ball bearings on the slippery vinyl seat cover; and Jocelyn was slowly sliding under the dashboard. It was no wonder she was holding onto Ray and Larry.

Butler kept right on talking to himself. "Like you bring your girl flowers 'cause you played around with her best friend, well you feel better and she gets some flowers, so she feels good, everybody gets something. If you hadn't been playin' around no one would have gotten anything, absolutely zero. So you screw around a bit, make up for it, and everybody gets somethin', everybody's happy. Like some rich guy, he screws people you know then turns around and gives them a bank or something, a library, yeah, and everyone's happy, that's the system man . . ."

Ray held onto Jocelyn with all his strength. He leaned against the door and stretched his head out the open window. He often saw dogs sticking their heads out of car windows and opening their mouths to the flow of air. He wondered if he could do that. Opening his mouth, Ray gagged on the onrush of warm air and insects, and Jocelyn slipped out of his grip. She slid completely under the dashboard, a huge mound of clothing stuck between a fence of legs, the gear shift, and the flapping glove compartment door. Jocelyn finally somehow squirmed around so that her legs were draped over Ray's and her head was propped against the floorboard. Temporarily saved from drowning in clothes, she gave a worried and exhausted smile. Butler continued talking to himself.

"It's the people that think they are doin' good, like those hippies, see they mess it up 'cause they don't give anything to anybody, always thinkin' they're better than anybody never makin' mistakes, you know, but you gotta make mistakes, screw up, do some bad stuff, 'cause then you try to make up for it and buy somethin' nice for someone and well that's what makes people happy—gettin' things—right? And you got somethin', right—vacation, swimmin' pool, remember, and I taught you baseball, out and safe and seein' Mexico, everybody gets something . . ."

They Could Have Ended Up In Argentina

<u>March 2, 1972</u>
Martinez, Raymond
#03-016-9657

<u>QUARTERLY REPORT</u>
     The Rogers have returned to the Burr residence. They report an incredible story about being in Mexico with some hippies and a sacrifice. Mrs. Rogers claims that she and Mr. Rogers learned to hitchhike by waving their thumbs in the air and cars stopped for them. Mrs. Rogers complained to me for an hour about not being able to take off her clothes,

that "they" had tied them on her. And Mrs. Burr just laughs at the story, saying, "It's a good thing they were faced in the right direction, or they could have ended up in Argentina!"

I do not know how much of this story to believe; they talk about stabbing tires with kitchen knives and leaving behind a rock collection worth a fortune. If any of their story is true, then Raymond Martinez has been abducted by his guardian. But according to the Rogers, the Raymond they speak of in Mexico can drive a truck, speaks to Indians, and plays baseball with a little league team. It's all quite impossible to believe. What is critical at this point is that Raymond is missing and we don't know his present location or if he is safe or in danger.

PLAN OF ACTION

I've written to Raymond's guardian and informed him that I must know Raymond's current address and living conditions. I have informed the guardian by mail that all ATD checks will be withdrawn until this office receives that information.

I telephoned Mr. Wilkins, the lawyer who arranged the guardianship for Raymond, and Mr. Kopecki, the lawyer for the stepmother that shares an inheritance with Raymond, and informed them of Raymond's absence.

Mr. Wilkins insisted that his clients John Henry Butler and Mrs. Burr are responsible for the care of Mr. Martinez and the protection of his inheritance. That they have established a trust fund for Raymond and it's quite possible that Mr. Butler is simply taking Raymond on a vacation. He chided me for not thinking that "handicapped people might need a vacation from bureaucrats." Mr. Wilkins also commented on government harassing citizens when they don't need help and being absent when they are needed. He also complained that this case was for him a "public defender job" and his fee was set at one hundred fifty dollars and he had other cases to worry about.

The lawyer for the stepmother said he talked with the stepmother and she thought Raymond might be with his aunt. She was anxious to sell their joint property and had found a buyer. Mr. Kopecki said he was conducting this business of a sale with Mr. Wilkins.

TRANSFER OF CASE

Supervisors in eligibility aren't sure if this case "at this time" warrants departmental investigation. The eligibility office is phasing out and doesn't want a backlog of cases. They recommend that J. B. Carver not proceed with this case—that the case be given to the Public Guardian in the district attorney's office or shifted to the jurisdiction of protective services division.

3/2/72 (Call with Mr. Lewis)

The Public Guardian in the D.A.'s office will not look at this case because the client already has a legal guardian and legal representation. They are overloaded and "will only take a case on the mandate of the court."

3/2/72 (Lunch with Ellis)

Protective Services in the DPSS doesn't know (with the new federal guidelines still pending) who has authorization to process this case. If the case is to be handled, they want to set up a review committee with the Public Guardian and representatives of DPSS.

You Have To Believe In God, He'll Kill You

March 15, 1972

"Ever seen a bank robbery, well watch closely." Butler was driving with one hand and pointing out "easy living" with the other. Butler seemed happy to be in Uruapan. Even if the city was a sixty-mile drive from the trailer park at Tingubatu, it was the closest city; and it felt wonderful to be away from the trailer park's drying loneliness. They drove down Uruapan's boulevards and across intersections, then back around the central plaza. Slowly circling the business section of the city like a four-wheeled shark. Finally, Butler parked, then propped both feet on the dashboard. When Ray tried to do the same, his shoes kept slipping. So Butler snapped open the glove compartment—a perfect rest for Ray's dusty tennis shoes.

"Watch the church over there and I'll tell you how we're gonna rob ourselves a bank." Butler twisted Ray's head toward the church and continued. "See those kids selling flowers?" Ray nodded yes. "Keep watching, there, see that—now tell me what did you see?"

Ray answered, "People go in the church like that and—"

"No, no," Butler admonished. "See the kids there sellin' the flowers right, then the old people take the flowers into the church and there—when the old folks leave, the kids go in and get the flowers so they can sell them all over again. Not bad for kids." Ray agreed by clapping his raised feet. Butler was still talking. "That's what we're going to do."

With a big grin, Ray picked up his guitar and started to open the truck door. "Hold it, hold it right there," Butler advised. "You expect to go singing your way into that bank, no siree, besides that guitar of yours looks like a purple machine gun." Ray carefully tucked the guitar under the front seat of the truck. "That's better." Butler glowed. "Let's go rob ourselves a bank."

Butler and Raymond Martinez entered the largest bank in Uruapan—Banco de Americas. A sign in the window brought a smile to Butler's face. He patted the sign as one would tap the fanny of a beautiful woman. Ray peered at the sign but couldn't decipher its meaning. U.S. CITIZENS WELCOME.

A massive safe of metal knobs and hinges sat in the rear of the bank like a squatting sun god. The face of the god was a giant steering wheel. On this day, the sun god was smiling. Like most gods, this one proved to be smiling out of the side of its mouth. Butler whispered to Ray, "See it's open for us, tellin' us to come on in and help ourselves." Ray was awed by the size of the gold door and by the inscriptions that covered it. The hollow sounds inside the bank. Hushed conversation. Like prayer.

In addition to the usual counter service, the interior of the bank was broken into a dozen private cubicles. An impeccably dressed bank official sat behind a large desk in each of these stalls. Flower arrangements graced each desk. And balusters around them smelled of waxed wood. And the air was cooler than outside and seemed tinted blue.

Butler surveyed the stalls, then swung open the low mahogany door of the first one and seated himself and Raymond inside. The officer greeted them cordially. Butler removed the last hundred-dollar bill from his wallet and requested traveler's checks. The bank official handled this quickly, then rose to shake Ray's and Butler's hands as they were leaving. Outside the bank, Butler turned to Ray and gloated. "It cost us twenty pesos for these traveler's checks. Say, in about four hours, we are going to lose them and collect another hundred bucks." Butler skipped and cheered. "Piece of cake."

Ray skipped and repeated, "Pie and cake."

The two friends walked around the park and down the shady side of the streets. Butler was excited. His walk was loose; his arms swung easily at his sides. He had so much to do, so much to teach Ray.

It was then that Butler noticed Ray's silence—it was like a sponge. Whenever Ray wanted to be still or tried to think or to express himself, he seemed to get lost and sad. Butler couldn't stand this. So he filled the painful stillness with a flurry of words. "Come on, those old folks and us, it wasn't goin' to work, they were just, hell, they spent all our money." Butler turned to Ray and made a funny face—pulled his tongue out of his mouth and rolled his eyes. "Doesn't anything make you smile?"

Ray tried to tell Butler how he felt, but it didn't come out right. "Larry had a radio . . ."

Butler angrily interrupted. "All they had was rocks, shit I don't know, you and I, man we're troopin' down here, here in the promised land with *señoritas*, you know fancy skirts all over waitin' to lift, and those old biddies—hell, you want to spend the rest of your life watchin' them pick up rocks? 'Sides, they wanted to go home."

As Butler spoke, his voice and his feet danced with increasing speed, until he was several steps in front of Ray and talking back over his shoulder. To catch up, Ray took a couple of skips that sent him bouncing in front of Butler. Butler's words followed Ray like a volley of Ping-Pong balls.

"Yeah, they, Jocelyn, she told me, you weren't there, she told me, yeah, that she had to get back to San Francisco that her checks were there—hey man, don't go walkin' in front of me, are you listenin' to me?"

Butler circled and faced Ray. Now he was out of patience. Ray had insulted him. Words busted out of his mouth in a spray of spit. "Where the Christ you goin'?"

Ray stopped. Frozen. He stared at the ground to avoid Butler's anger. Butler couldn't stand being ignored.

"Man I've been doin' a lot for you, you know I got some big plans for us livin' down here, the two of us and what is this you walkin' away from me and everythin'. Jump it, I bust my brains hustlin' and now this, what is this— Look at me when I'm talkin' to you."

Butler kicked at the ground like an enraged baseball manager. A veil of dirt spread over Ray's shoes. From the center of this dust swirl the tirade continued.

"Tyin' your shoes, makin' sure you get somethin' to eat. You think it's some kind of party? Now I need you, you know, want some kinda help in this bank, and—oh yeah, you go mushing on me—well I could leave you too, I don't need you—you got that! Bam I'm off, by myself, not pullin' you, teachin' you everything, always answerin' your goddam questions— Where are you going?

Now ask, now ask it. When I want you to, go on and ask— Where are we going?"

"Where are we going?" Ray stuttered.

A little shocked, Butler looked up and down the street. The truth was he really didn't know where they were going. He pointed across the street to a cemetery so he could salvage his authority. "There—we're goin' over there and get us some rest in the shade."

Butler grumbled in a low voice as they crossed the street. "You know, you got it made, nobody takes care of me, you hear that, course not . . ."

"Yeah."

Butler nodded his head the way Ray does and eased. "Yeah," he said in a voice like Ray's. Then, absorbed in thought, blurted it out. "You're right about the radio, though."

Their conversation was like a tennis game. Except that no service ever went from the server to the other player's court. Butler served. "The radio, we shoulda kept the radio!"

Ray tried a return. "Where are we going, John Henry, huh, where are we going?"

La Omnipresencia De Dios

White adobe shrines with ornate iron teeth smiled at the two men as they approached the land where the dead are alive. Crosses made of tinfoil shimmered as if about to take flight, while garlands of decaying flowers tilted and sagged like worn-out halos. The air was dry and dusty. It strangled conversation. Forced their thoughts toward the ceramic angels with their cracked and crumbling outstretched arms and the plastic flowers in rusting coffee cans. Toward the shrines, with their shelves of fading photographs. Toward a lace fan propped against the statue of the Virgin Mary. What did that mean? Or the doll placed next to a small mound of earth? They listened to the whispers of the living dead.

For Ray and Butler, in this maze of stone, time stopped. The sun was straight overhead. A time that the Aztec call the time of truth. A time in which shadow and life are one. Standing in the center of the cemetery, Ray and Butler found themselves facing a small domed building. The structure was open on all four sides and painted a chalklike pastel blue that seemed to blend in with the sky. An inscription was painted in gold letters around the outer rim of the dome:

LA OMNIPRESENCIA DE DIOS

For the Aztec, this cupola was the "seeing-eye portal." The place to visit the dead, visit life. To be in the presence of God.

The wrought-iron gate to the portal was leaning— held open by the grasp of a gnarled tree. The cool shadow within the rotunda beckoned. In the center of the floor were two wooden kneeling posts. Ray and Butler entered. Inside, calmed by their surroundings, both were content to simply sit in the bath of cool air. Ray curled on the cement floor, while Butler propped himself against one of the prayer stands.

This solitude was something new for the travelers. In all their time together they had never been in a place of quiet. For the first time Butler did not have to fend off the world, scheme, or pretend. There was no need. And as for Ray, well, in this place of ghosts his perception was sharpened. For once, much that he felt and imagined was verified. The portal of life gave these men a chance together. Butler could slow down, and Ray could be alive with visions.

Butler took a knife from his pocket and pointed at the field of crosses. "Do you believe in God?" he asked in a somber tone. "Does it bother you this stealin' stuff?"

"You have to believe in him, he'll kill you—" Ray said with great confidence.

"I mean, do you think there's a God lookin' at us right now, keepin' score sorta, you know?"

"I don't know he just saves your life, has a birthday party—"

"Birthday party?"

"Birthday party in heaven for you and sees you when you're sleeping."

"Oh yeah," Butler murmured and pointed the knife blade at Ray— "And what do you think of me?"

"You're my friend!" said Ray proudly. "My best friend."

Butler jabbed the point of his knife into the prayer stand and began to carve his name. "Hey, you know?" he said carefully. His words were punctuated by the slow twisting of the knife. "I got a peek at your records, yeah when they made me your guardian—you didn't tell me you were busted for stealin'—you shouldn't you know think of me as your friend. Oh, I like you, don't get me wrong, but, well, I'm, it's— I'm not all uh, you know like in those movies, cowboy movies—"

Ray jerked to attention, sat upright. "I watch *Gunsmoke* right after *I Love Lucy*. *I Love Lucy* is at three—*Gunsmoke*, *I Love Lucy*, and *Eight is Enough*. The horses are like Jake—"

"Yeah, yeah, well, you remember how in the westerns well the bank robbers—"

"Bad guys get shot, you know."

"Wait, you got caught stealin' play money from Woolworths, right?"

"It was a lot of money, this much." Ray bundled his arms around an imaginary package.

"Well, if you had a partner, see like me—"

"We're partners!" Ray glowed.

"Yeah, if we pulled off this bank job, well like in the westerns, the two bad guys, that's us—well we gotta split up, you know, you ride one way, and me another." Butler completed carving his name.

Ray was just beginning to dream. "We don't have horses. Jake is a horse I feed him doughnuts he likes doughnuts, horses like doughnuts—"

"Are you listenin' to me?" Butler closed his knife and turned to Ray. "You see, we go hide different places. And the cops, they can't find us, 'cause they're lookin' for two guys not one. You understand?"

"We don't have no horses—" Ray pondered. "No doughnuts neither—"

"What do you mean?" Butler smiled. "What do you call these?" Butler tapped his wooden prayer stand as one would pat the rump of a great stallion. "I hereby call this here horse of mine—Nellie Bell—no that's no—"

"Thunderbolt!" Ray yelled.

"No, how about Lightning, no I call this horse of mine—Hey! Yeah! I call this horse Burr . . . ito!"

Ray laughed. "You riding that old lady, she's not so fast—"

"So what's your horse?" Butler asked his companion as he straddled the wooden stand.

Ray slapped his legs over the stall and almost fell over. "Thunderbolt no—Jake—Thunderbolt Jake!"

"Yahoo!" Butler yelped like a cowboy. "Let's get out of here!"

The two men bounced up and down and leaned forward, allowing their wooden horses to stretch into a gallop. They bobbed down an imaginary hill, splashed across a river, and raced into an opening. "Look behind us, oh no it can't be." Butler motioned to his hard-riding companion. "Look—the sheriff and his posse!"

Ray glanced over his shoulder, and both men started shooting at their pursuers with fingertip six-shooters.

"Bang, bang— Got one, bang— Bang!"

Butler contorted his body to shoot under the belly of his horse. It was his trademark—making the easy difficult.

"Bang, bang, bang!"

While Ray tried to duplicate the trick shot, Butler made believe that he'd been hit. He straightened up in his saddle and then slumped forward. "They got me in the shoulder—keep going!"

Ray decided he'd help his friend. He leaped from his wooden seat and tried to straddle Butler's mount. Which didn't work. Ray ended up falling backward and to one side. Of course he had both hands on Butler's shoulders and was pulling Butler backward with him. Butler was laughing and yelling, "Not me—get them!"

Ray twisted to take one last shot. That did it! Both men collapsed in a heap on the cement floor. Only now Butler was pretending he was the sheriff. "Got you! You low-down bank robber—got you at last!"

Ray rolled over and tried to squirm away, but Butler wouldn't let him escape. The two men crunched together and tumbled across the floor.

Butler found Ray's ticklish spot, and Ray was laughing so hard it became contagious.

"Pleeeese not there, o, o, ah, not ha, ha, o oh, eee, pl, plee,—na, na, ho, ho . . ."

Both men were now giggling, tickling each other, rolling on the ground.

Later, lying apart—lying on their backs, wiping the tears from their eyes—trying to stop the earthquake in their stomachs—that's when they noticed someone was watching them. The sight sobered them.

"Oh no!" Ray said. "Look up there."

Butler's mouth dropped open. Above them, in the curvature of the ceiling, was a universe of eyes. A thousand pastel eyes glared upon them. Painted eyes with garish lashes that accentuated their expression of pain and searching. Accompanying this floating cosmos of eyes were crude illustrations of places between life and death. Planets, pyramids, and volcanoes seemed to dance and spin. Skeletons kicked at glaring eyes. An inscription was at the center of the dome—like the dome's pupil. That's it, the entire ceiling was a giant eye. With his inscription staring earthward.

ESPERAMOS LA RESURECCIÓN DE LOS MUERTOS

Ray could translate that, though where this translation came from he couldn't know. As a child, he had attended church, and his aunt had spoken Spanish—but that was so long ago. Ray spoke quietly. "We hope for—"

Butler was not pleased. Ray was showing something that Butler didn't have. "Come on, what you doin'? You tellin' me you know what that gibberish up there means? Come on let's get out of here." Butler stood up angrily as Ray remained entranced by the vision on the ceiling. "Come on—get up!"

Ray continued. "We hope for the resurrection—"

Again, Butler interrupted. "Resurrection, what's that, you mean you are readin' even know what the shit, hell, you have. You don't know the when or how of it—resurrection—come on, come on man, I'm tellin' you get your ass up we're gettin' out of here!"

Ray pointed to the message above them. Pointed to each word and repeated, "We hope for the resurrection of the dead."

Butler joked, "And we hope for lots of erections for hot and pretty jean eaters and lots of money from this here local bank job and—"

Ray finally stood. "It means that the dead come here."

"It means!" Butler pushed Ray out of the portal. "It means we're gettin' out of here, spooky crappy place—" Butler kicked Ray in the seat of the pants— "And I don't want you goin' fancy on me—you gotta remember who's boss, who runs this here show, who takes care of you— isn't that right?"

Ray was gazing over his shoulder at the small sky-blue building as Butler yanked him into the yard of stone. Ray smiled. He thought his friend was continuing their game, but Butler didn't want to play anymore. He didn't like Ray knowing things. Showing off. Being superior. So he went on another roll.

"You know what you are, stop smilin' at me—you're a dumb shit, you know what I mean, Jesus, you don't know the difference between what was that erection yeah you don't know the meanin' of it—shit you ever had a girl—those jean eaters, I hate them. They tease you, you know—I want, but I don't—so you get mixed up. They don't give a shit, no one gives a shit. Stop smilin' at me."

Once again the words came like a rainstorm. Too many words. Too many feelings to decipher. Ray pulled within himself. He was used to that. He listened to his own breathing and waited for the storm to pass.

"You go around all day with that smile on your face and that question, always askin' the same thing—with that shit-eating smile. People like you—walk right up to you and talk to you—jean-eaters, good-lookin' jean eaters. Goddam they all just walk right up to you, people like you, take care of you. Like me, I don't know why I'm doin' this shit—the money isn't there anymore. You're a dumb shit. Can't do nothin' for yourself—nobody takes care of me. Nobody. Nobody likes me, you hear that. Not in school, not there, they hate you in school—if you talk out you know, or don't know the answers to their dumb questions. And Mrs. Burr, damn, boy, she doesn't give a hot shit . . ."

Ray tried to reach out and hug Butler. As Butler jerked away, Ray stammered, "I, I like you."

Butler was infuriated. "You don't count! Look at you, can't tie your shoes, you piss in your pants, can't make it with women—man I don't want you for a friend, you hear me, understand—you're not my friend, you're nobody."

Ray understood rejection. Yes, it was familiar. Butler turning away. Spitting words. Not wanting to be touched. Ray saw his mother and the candles on his birthday cake. But no one was coming. That's what she said. She was crying. "No one was coming to his birthday but God has birthday parties in heaven for all those that miss them on earth!" Ray felt the tides in his body rush to his head. He felt himself shaking. And uncontrollably crying. He felt ashamed. But couldn't stop. A grown man that can ride a horse and has a friend was standing in the middle of a cemetery and crying.

Butler was equally shaken. "Come on, come on, I

didn't mean all that, shit, of course you're my friend, haven't we been through a lot together, and didn't I teach, hey, who let you drive the truck, yeah that's better and didn't I teach you to pitch a fast ball, course, that's better, much better." As Butler spoke, he surveyed the graveyard. A scheme was hatching in his head. Perhaps he didn't need Ray any longer. He surely didn't need this blubbering idiot standing in front of him and sobbing.

"Say Ray," Butler said. "I got this game, you want to play another game? It's kinda like that western you know—"

Ray shook his head yes. His face brightened with anticipation. "The game we're going to play—sure you want to? It's called hide-and-seek!"

Ray liked that. He would enjoy another game. His tears left, and he began to twitch expectantly. And to stomp up and down.

"Ya gotta go to the bathroom?" Butler asked.

Ray shook his head no and continued his rhythmless dance.

"Good, then this is how you play—you go hide someplace, you see and I count to ten, then I try to come and find you—"

Ray's dance shook his whole body. He was smiling and shaking. Butler knew why Ray was anxious. Ray either had to piss, or else he was so excited that he'd talk about the game for the next three months. Nothing with Ray was easy.

"Well, go on," Butler said, pointing. "What are you waitin' for? You're supposed to hide, you know, uhm, get out of here, go where I can't see you."

Smiling, Ray pointed to himself. "Do you understand, shit?" Butler asked impatiently.

Ray answered with confidence. "Yes!"

"Well, then do it. Go hide someplace and I'll count to ten, okay what the fuck—" Butler grabbed Ray's hand and walked him toward one of the burial chambers. The chamber was a miniature church with windows and a small altar. "Here," Butler explained, "you hide in here—and then I'll come and find you." Butler had Ray squat on the floor of the memorial. The chamber was very small—barely enough room for the two men and the protruding ledges with their treasures of statuary, vases, and stubs of countless candles. The pungent smell of decaying flowers mingled with the sweeter aroma of bottled lavender. Lizards scurried for shelter. Butler stood at the entrance to the chamber and gave a final order. "Now don't move till I come and find you—you got that?"

Ray smiled happily. "I hide real good, don't find me."

Butler turned his back on Ray's grinning face and walked briskly toward the cemetery gate. Ray's voice echoed after him.

"I hide real good!"

Butler approached the gate and paused. He looked back at the memorial and sighed. Then, just as he was about to leave, a hand reached out and grabbed him.

"I found you!"

It was Ray, beaming from ear to ear.

"I found you!"

Butler was more than surprised. His heart pounded, and a trace of morning's breakfast climbed into his nose. He beat Ray's hand off his shoulder with a shrill cry. "Never do that again, scarin' me, fuck scarin' the shit out of me—" Before he could continue, he found himself breaking into a nervous laugh. Ray was standing with both hands covering his eyes.

"I hide really good, don't find me."

"Oh shit!" Butler exhaled. Then studied the man in front of him. A man with both hands pressed against his eyes. Hands that masked a familiar smile. Butler repeated, "Oh shit," and slowly walked Ray back to the center of the cemetery. Ray walked with both hands over his eyes.

"All right, good," Butler instructed. "Now, you stand right here, just like you're doin', and keep your hands over your eyes. That's it. Now count real slow and I'll go hide—"

Ray started a troubled count. "One, one, two,

three—one, two, three, one, two, three, four, four, three—"

Butler, now sure Ray was keeping his eyes covered, briskly walked away. At the gate he looked back. Ray was standing and counting. Butler slowly trotted across the street and out of sight. Ray was still counting when Butler returned around the corner and looked again into the cemetery. Butler stared down the empty street and back into the cemetery at the stationary figure trying to count to ten. Under his breath Butler echoed Ray's efforts—one, two, three—and finally joined in and orchestrated the counting by loudly yelling, "Three, four, five, six—"

With Butler's assistance, Ray finished counting and took his hands from his eyes. He turned and spied full circle. No one was there! . . . But then he found his friend standing at the far corner of the cemetery fence. Ray ran. Almost stumbling into an open grave. Then stopped and put both hands over his eyes. A smile crept beneath the palms of his hands. Butler was crying—but could never let Ray see that. He was crying not in sympathy with the lonely man in front of him but for the loneliness in his own life. Butler studied his idiot friend standing at attention with both his eyes covered. Always smiling. This was his first and only friend. Butler dried his tears with a sweep of his sleeve and commanded in a loud voice, "Hey come on— say Ray—my man—we got us a bank to rob."

Tomorrow

Late-afternoon sun slanted through the high windows, giving the inside of the bank the look of a striped
T-shirt. Bands of light crossed above Ray and John Henry
and radiated off the massive safe. The door that had hung
so open in the morning was now shut tight. Noticing
Ray's fixation on the closed safe, Butler joked, "They
know we're coming." Butler waited until the stall they'd
been in before was free for business. The same friendly
official assumed his position behind the desk.

"What is it that I can do for you?" he asked.

Butler explained that their traveler's checks had
been lost or stolen and that he'd come to replace them.
The official asked for the serial numbers and left the
wooden enclosure.

In a few minutes, the official returned and asked
where the two were residing in Uruapan. Butler answered that they were traveling and planning to leave
that evening. The official rose with that information and
retired once again to the back of the bank. Butler assured
Ray. "It's the old car salesman trick, talk to the boss—you
know—intimidate the customer." Ray smiled.

A new official arrived. Older and dressed more ex-
pensively. He, too, was polite and offered apologies but
insisted, "Are you a regular customer of this bank? Or
perhaps you may know a regular customer?"

Butler blurted "No."

"I see," came a studied reply. Then, "I'm glad to tell
you that your money will be—tomorrow."

"Tomorrow!" Butler groaned and stood up.

"Tomorrow at this time we will have your money, or
perhaps it will be found, no?"

Disgusted, Butler banged the swinging door of the cubicle. Then—more frustration—he had to reach back and drag Ray through the bank.

The next morning the same scene was reenacted—like a grade B movie. Except that now a police inspector asked questions about their travel and how they lost the money. It was a strained conversation, with Butler bursting with accusations that the officials claimed not to understand. Everyone agreed to try to solve this matter—tomorrow.

Finally, there were no tomorrows left; at least that's what Butler reasoned. A senior bank official handed Butler a folder of forms. "*Señor*, when these are completed, then we will be able to process your claim." The forms were in Spanish. "To translate, you may use our service in booth number four. There is a fee of thirty pesos."

"Thirty pesos!" Butler roared. All he had left in his pocket were traveler's checks, the very traveler's checks he was claiming were lost. And the forms. They looked more menacing than anything from the DPSS. Butler's fears squirmed through his lips. "Hell, take some college professor to figure this out, I haven't got time for this."

The official accepted the return of the packet. "As you wish, *señor*. If you change your mind, we will be open—tomorrow."

That Was A Good Baseball Game

April 26, 1972
The pickup bucked like a wild horse down the dirt road. "Sit down! Sit down! Jesus Christ, sit down!" Butler was yelling as he drove. Ray and three frightened passengers were bouncing and rolling around the back of the truck. "Here, do I turn here? Oh Jesus, look out!" The truck went sprawling over a drain ditch. The jolt threw all the passengers backward. Butler hit the brake. "All right, everybody out!" Butler shouted. Ray and the three passengers jumped from the truck, relieved to be on firm land. "Ray," Butler commanded, "ask them where it was we were supposed to be drivin' them." Ray looked dumfounded. The three passengers pointed in three different directions. Butler's words collided with a wave of Spanish. "You were supposed to hit the top of the truck," he demonstrated with his hand pounding the top of the cab. "That means stop! You didn't hit, now we're lost." The three passengers began hitting the side of the cab and pointing in all directions. Ray did likewise. That was enough.

Butler grabbed Ray and threw him into the cab of the truck. Almost smashed the WHIZ guitar. Butler slammed his door, and with a cloud of dust, the Butler Trucking Company left behind their first customers. Butler was laughing and shaking, trying to tell Ray about "the funny guys flyin' around when we hit the drain back there." Ray was checking his guitar, making sure it survived what Butler called "big business."

"Turn up the radio, that's it. Let it blast!" Latin music rumbled through the pickup and into the street. "Louder!" Butler yelped. Ray turned the dial and scurried around the front of the truck. "See, see, I told you," Butler was congratulating himself. "It's working!" Indian merchants on their morning trek to market waved. Butler used his pickup Spanish. *"Aquí! Aquí!"* Indians converged around the truck. Butler launched into his prepared speech as if he were running for mayor. "So the truck here, with this big bed—you get to ride and the truck carries all your stuff. Do you understand? And you pay us—" The crowd dispersed like water going around a rock in a stream. Butler was confused and hurt. "Turn it off, turn it off." Ray climbed into the truck and turned the radio louder. Then he found off. Butler was confounded.

"I thought I had it all figured out, you know, like the jitneys on Mission Street. See" —Butler pointed— "like those 'peso taxis' that run up and down the boulevard. Hell, we've got truck space, can carry more than any of those buggers and you can't get lost going up and—" Butler was tracking a "peso taxi" as it rumbled down the street. "That's what we need," Butler said with excitement. "See all that shit, it's magic, we've got to appeal to these people on their own, you know paint the truck and put some flowers and lights around, why didn't I see that—it's advertising!"

The flowers came from the park, "free for the picking," in Butler's words. The Christmas lights were Ray's discovery. He spotted them in an outdoor booth and with Butler's help wired them to the truck's generator and strung them around the back window of the pickup. The final touch of magic was to name the truck. All the "peso taxis" in Uruapan seemed to have names emblazoned in shells or colorful buttons. Not to be outdone, Butler painted BUTLER TRUCKING on "his" door. And Ray selected ELVIS for his motto. The partners shook hands, praised their cunning, and set off to try again.

"Turn it up, that's got it," Butler ordered. "Now—do it now." Ray followed a carefully rehearsed routine: When Butler signaled, he leaped onto the back of the truck and sang his Elvis Presley songs. Ray was an instant hit. Indians, tourists, merchants, gathered to see Elvis. Even a religious procession with papier-mâché saints, priests in golden hats, and a platoon of uniformed children—all came to a halt at the sight of the man singing in the back of the pickup.

It was the way he was singing that mattered. The heartfelt truth he showed. The music didn't matter . . . It wasn't very good. The lyrics were all mixed up. That didn't matter. There was something special happening on the apron of the pickup. A chant from the past. A glory and innocence long lost. Ray did his posing, shooting one arm in the air. Spreading his feet. Holding the guitar over his head. He could feel the audience. Their excitement gave him more energy and encouragement. He sang louder. Played harder.

> *One for the money*
> *Two for the show*
> *Three to get ready*
> *Now go cats go*
> *And don't you*
> *Step on my blue suede shoes*
> *You can do anything*
> *But—*

For the Aztec, the retarded child was special. Here on this earth to remind us of the songs in our heart. The eyes of these children are not clouded by greed or envy. They do not betray the heart. They give their pure selves. Sing songs. Make the heart happy.

Ray was winding up. Jumping, almost falling. Smiling and laughing. Then turning serious and singing his loudest. Giving it his best. The crowd was now at one with the performance. Sharing the joy of the song and this gift to life. Flowers were thrown at Ray as he finished his song. A small girl placed a bouquet of carnations on the tailgate, a few coins bounced on the metal flooring of the truck. Ray was into his fourth bow. Thanking everyone. Trying to hug the small girl who gave the flowers.

Butler was blinded by the humiliation of it. He

jumped back onto the back of the truck and snatched the guitar from Ray's hands. "What the hell is going on?" he cried. "Don't you people see this is a business, we're here waitin' to drive you, transport goods—can't you see," he pointed to the side of the truck. "Butler Trucking." The yelling drove a knife into the crowd. They fell silent, wheeled around, stepped back, walked away, looking over their shoulders at this raving gringo. And Ray stood there, helpless, powerless, stripped of his magic and power. Butler was still furious, even after the crowd had retreated. "I don't know, man, I ask you to do a simple thing—sing a song, tried to do you a favor, make you feel good. You can't sing worth shit but I thought, give you some fun, make it fun. I don't get it—you're not supposed to stop traffic with that, just get us a few customers."

Before he knew what he was doing, Butler raised the guitar and smashed it against the pavement. The strings snapped and flailed like whips, and the plastic heart splintered. Butler crashed the guitar again and again against the curb. This time he knew what he was doing. In slow motion, pieces of plastic scattered into the air. And the word WHIZ disintegrated. His fury spent, Butler dropped the arm of the guitar into the gutter. Ray tried to pick up the broken heart and reflector buttons, but Butler wouldn't let him. "Forget it, get off the ground. Leave that alone. We're getting out of here." Ray hid one reflector button in the clutch of his hand. Later, he placed it in the pocket of his bathing suit.

They drove for several hours into the sun. Then, after a while, the sun was at their backs. Butler didn't say a word. And Ray knew it wasn't the time to speak. He fell into a trance as the truck crossed the landscape. Clothes drying on great racks waved as they passed. And travelers on the road—everything seemed to be moving. Changing. The sky, the road, the mountains. Everything was moving and changing. The earth turned from dark black to rust red. Vegetation from green to brown. The truck seemed to be moving faster and faster. As if on the fragile rim of some swirling vortex—the tires sounded like stones raining on the earth.

The truck finally came to a stop at a gas station in a small town six hours' drive from Uruapan. Butler stopped the engine. They sat together in silence for a few minutes. Painful silence. Then Butler muttered something Ray didn't understand. "That was a good baseball game."

"What?" Ray asked.

"I want you to go over and get us a map so we can figure out where we are." Butler's voice was flat.

Ray got out of the truck and walked into the gas-station office. He was wearing his San Francisco Giant baseball cap, checkered bathing suit, and tennis shoes. When he turned around, the pickup was gone.

Watch Out For The Man With The Thin Tie

April 26, 1972
Martinez, Raymond
#03-016-9657

SUMMARY OF SERVICES

The department received word in February that John Henry Butler had taken two other ATD clients along with Raymond to Mexico. The clients are Larry and Jocelyn Rogers. Butler was trying to arrange guardianship for them, it said. When their ATD checks didn't come in February, Butler waited awhile and then finally left the Rogers out on the main highway in Mexico and without any belongings, money, or transportation back to the United States. They did hitchhike back to San Francisco and reported all of this information to the department. They are now living again in Mrs. Burr's board-and-care home.

Raymond's ATD checks have been held for February, March, and April, and I sent a letter to Butler and explained that I would have to see him and Raymond in person so a plan for the administration of Raymond's finances and living arrangements could be made. I received a letter from Butler dated March 14, 1972 (see attachment) stating that Raymond was going to remain in Mexico and he no longer wanted to receive any ATD. The letter was signed by Butler, and Raymond's signature appears at the bottom. I fear that Raymond is not receiving the best care and that his life could be in danger. On the letter I received from Butler, there was no return address in Mexico, and the address on the envelope was the San Francisco answering service.

Mr. Wilkins, the attorney for Butler, reported to

my supervisor that Bank of America told him that checks have been returned to the bank and Raymond's signature had been forged. Wilkins asked if the department could pay for his continued services on this case since he had spent so much time on it. I explained that the Department of Social Services couldn't pay for any of his services and that this was a matter that was between Wilkins, Raymond, and Butler.

A meeting was held in the city attorney's office with Mr. Wilkins. Also present were Juris Kopecki, attorney for Raymond Martinez's stepmother, John Dillon, Roger Geoffrey, and Con Shea of the guardian's office. At this meeting we discussed the possibility of guardianship on Raymond Martinez being lifted because Butler was found to be an unfit person for the guardianship of Raymond Martinez. Plans have been talked about to have Raymond and Butler go to the Mexican consulate and at that time possibly have the United States step in and bring Raymond back to this country to live. This was talked about at the meeting, but then it was decided that this plan would not be feasible and was not carried out. It was definitely decided to have the guardianship lifted for Raymond.

Mr. Wilkins filed petition #19720 for a removal of guardian and for suspension of guardian's power, pending the hearing (see attached document). Judge Byron Arnold signed these papers in Superior Court, and they are dated 4/13/72. The actual hearing for removal is set for 6/9/72 at 10:30 A.M. in Superior Court.

If and when Raymond is returned to the United States, his ATD case will then be reopened, and I will, at that time, assist in trying to locate a board-and-care home where Raymond can live. Raymond is not capable of handling his own affairs or living on his own, and I feel a board-and-care arrangement would be the best situation for him if he is returned to the United States. The case is being sent as per supervisor's request to the D.A.'s office for review.

Croce, 4/26/72

Re: Raymond Martinez
#03-016-9657

Dear Mrs. Ellis:

In reply to your letter of March 6, 1972, I have talked to Raymond in regard to his wishes, he would like to stay and live in Mexico, I explained that his welfare checks would be stopped, but that I believed he could get along very nicely on the soc sec plus the rent money he receives. He says he does not wish to ever return to the United States as there is nothing there that interests him other than one friend, whom is joining us here in Mexico. As to my business, it can be operated anywhere as long as a San Francisco address is maintained (1322 Noriega).

I believe this change would be benifisual to the health and welfare of Raymond, here he is not looked down appon and is able to learn easer due to his Spanish background. Living and everything is very cheap here, we are having a two bedroom house built for less than $5000.00

Raymond has met a very nice young lady who he may marry. I have told him to wait a few months before he decides. As to his finances, he is far better off here than in the U.S. when he was placed on A.T.D. I believe. This was a very harmful thing to have been done to Raymond. He is not totally disabled and was working in a gas station at the time, he was made to quit this job. He has several ableities he is very musically inclined, and I have bought him a good electrical gitar and amplifier he plays by ear, as he is unable to read notes. He is also capable of handleing gas station work, is a fair mechanic. I am sure that I can get him a job with Pemix, here in Mexico. His main difficulty is reading and writing but does not seem to have trouble learning in Spanish.

I hope this will releve your mind as to Raymonds welfare. He is by far better off than he ever was and is now his own man, with a little supervision and help from me.

Thanking you in advance for your help to Raymond in the past.

Sincerely,

John H. Butler
      Guardian of Raymond Martinez

P.S. This has been read to Raymond in full.

IN THE SUPERIOR COURT OF THE STATE OF CALIFORNIA IN AND FOR THE CITY AND COUNTY OF SAN FRANCISCO

In the Matter of the Estate and Guardianship of	))) No. 1201
RAYMOND MARTINEZ,	)) DECLARATION RE MAILING
an Incompetent Person.	))

Jonathan R. Wilkins declares as follows:

By reason of the interest of the parties listed below in the matter of the Estate and Guardianship of Raymond Martinez, an Incompetent Person, I have this date mailed a copy of the Petition for Removal of Guardian and the Order Suspending Powers of Guardian Pending Hearing on the Petition for Removal, and a Notice of Time and Place of Hearing on said Petition, to each of the following named persons at their respective addresses shown:

Mr. John Dillon, Supervisor
Service Unit
San Francisco Social Service
585 Bush Street
San Francisco, California

Mr. Roger W. Geoffrey
Assistant Manager-
  Operations
Bank of America
Divisadero-Hayes Branch
560 Divisadero Street
Box 37001
San Francisco, California
  94137

Mr. Con S. Shea
Public Guardian of the
  City and County of
  San Francisco
Attention: W. F. Minton,
  Esq.
1212 Market Street
San Francisco, Califor-
  nia 94102

On this date I also mailed true copies of all the aforementioned documents, together with Citation to said hearing, to John Henry Butler, also known as John H. Butler, at the following addresses:

970 Fulton Street, San Francisco, California
1322 Noriega Street, San Francisco, California
c/o Lista de Correos, Euruapan, Michoacán,
  Mexico

Executed in San Francisco, California, on April 14th, 1972.

I declare under penalty of perjury that the above and foregoing is true and correct.

_____
Valerie Ann Morris

Sherry showed the documents to J. B. Carver. "That's what I had to do," she complained. "They want me to close the case!" Carver had seen this all before. "Everyone is bailing out, especially that lawyer Wilkins. He's a case. I talked with Mrs. Burr and she swears that Wilkins knew her son was an ex-convict and would be trouble. In fact, she claims it was their idea to have her as guardian but she became ill so junior was thrown in as a substitute." Miss Croce fidgeted with the documents. "I don't understand why the public guardian's office is dragging its heels—"

Before she could answer, Carver was explaining. "Lawyers, it's 'thin-tie time,' those boys are all after careers and your client, well let's face it, he isn't the kid of some wealthy family, or a Panther bust. Now, if he were Sally Stanford now that would get some headlines. No, they're going to sit on it, and hope it goes away. What I think—"

"What gets me," Sherry blurted, "is that no one wants to take responsibility for being Raymond's guardian. I mean Wilkins is doing everything possible to disassociate himself from the case and the D.A. doesn't want it and the guardian's office, some office, the only thing they take care of is coffee cups and meetings."

Carver took the documents from Miss Croce's trembling hands. "You can let go, it's only one client in a drawerful and—"

"What!" Sherry snapped. "I don't, can't let go, I didn't take this job to have coffee and play along."

"Then I'll tell you something." Carver aimed his eyes at hers. "This case you're chasing, everyone's telling you it's not important, but they're also telling you—lady get off it, don't rattle this case—send it to the D.A. and forget it."

"Do you believe that?"

"Do you?"

"I thought you were on my side in this one. What are you telling me?"

"I'm telling you that this can cost you, that's all I'm saying."

"No, no you don't get away that easy. I'm asking you—you what do you think? Are you going to help me or are you 'too busy' like everyone else?"

Carver grinned and tapped his fingers against his cheek—confirmations that he was working, not quitting. "Just checking up, that's all," he tried to joke. Then became serious. "So can you get a phone?"

"A phone?"

"Yeah. If our boy is in Mexico, then why not phone him and tell him to get home?"

"Are you serious?"

"It's the only way for now. Find a phone that you can run a bill on and get to work. Call the big hotels in the

major cities, travel bureaus, consulate offices—start
something happening. Call the police down there and
tell them you're some big-shot government official and
you want an "all points" on Raymond and Butler—that
might turn up a lead, and the banks, call the banks."
Miss Croce opened a note pad and made a careful shopping list under the title FIND RAYMOND MARTINEZ.

After she completed that, she turned to Carver.
"And what are you going to be doing?"

"My job is to help you keep your job," he said in a
half-serious tone, then quickly added, "I'm going to
check the banks here—you'd be surprised how money
leaves such a beautiful trail. And if you have time, keep
an eye on Mrs. Burr, visit her at least once a week, take
her a box of chocolates, and watch for clues—"

"Clues?" Croce interrupted.

"Yes, clues like extra furniture, letters, anything
from Butler—he's going to head home, I can feel it."

Dragonflies Are Sewing My Eyes Shut

April 27, 1972

Ray stood on the curb at the gas station. Watching.
Waiting. Surely Butler would come back. Ray felt the
sun against his back in the morning. And squinted into
its afternoon brilliance. Only a few cars took this road. A
bus passed going one way in the middle of the day and
returned past him late at night. He was warm during the
day and freezing at night. Still, he waited.

The gas-station owner was a man without teeth,
without hair, and without shoes. The only thing that

clung to him was the grease that made his hands look like huge black spiders. This man with black hands left for home at midday and returned to work in the early evening. Opened the station and closed it. Turned on the lights. Turned them off. He and Ray often looked at each other but said nothing. Reaching into his pocket, Ray found the reflector button from his guitar. He squeezed it. Then worried that Butler would take the button away when he returned.

Ray scratched the hard, crusty ground with a stick. The scratching gave the stick a sharp point. Lizards crawled across his lines and scampered away to wherever lizards went. Ray wondered where that was. Several large buzzards began to slowly circle above the place where Ray stood. Watching the birds' lazy flight made Ray dizzy. Sweat caked the corners of his mouth. It gave his tongue the flat taste of dust. Insects searching for moisture and a place to lay their eggs stung his underarms and crotch.

By shuffling his feet, Ray could erase the clay lines. Then he cut more lines with his stick. The point of the stick was alive and warm to the touch. And the marking in the dirt reminded Ray of his pen and the marks he'd made on his arm. He tried to make as many slashes as he could. That way he might summon an angry Mrs. Burr or John Henry. Angry was better than nothing. His skin itched, and he was hungry; but he was afraid to leave. Afraid that he'd miss Butler. He looked at the map. Folded it and stuffed it into his bathing-suit pocket. Took it out again. Wondered if he had gotten the wrong map. Returning the map to his pocket, he checked with his hand—the silver button was still in his pocket. And so was a book of matches.

Discomfort caused by overfull bowels and bladder had to be fought. Ray rocked on one leg, then another. Sat down on the curb. Stood up. Walked a few paces to a signboard. Then back. Watching the road. Waiting. Waiting for the sight of the pickup and the yellow trailer. The pickup with the door painted Elvis.

The welcome cool of early evening deepened into a chill. His body shook, and his breath turned into an icy cloud. One car passed. And the blue and white bus.

With the morning light, Ray watched and waited for the sun. It touched the mountains. Then crept downward, lighting the tops of telephone poles. Finally, the warmth of the sun fell earthward. It angled through the cactus and roadside sign, then splintered and cascaded across the roadway. The air became warm, full of light and flying things. Ray felt surrounded by their soft humming. A humming of insects on the move. Plants turning to the sun. Seeds in flight. Morning dew evaporating, billowing upward. The ground drying and pulling tight.

A piece of ribbon lay trapped on a thistle. Pink ribbon shiny in the morning light. It felt soft, winding around one finger. Then another. It felt good against his lips. He stuffed the ribbon in his pocket with the folded map. Then made sure the button was still at the bottom of his pocket. Fingered the matchbook.

Ray sat down, feeling warmed and comfortable. He propped his head against the road sign. Frightened that he might fall asleep, he jabbed his hand with burrs of the thistle. He watched a trickle of blood dry in his hand and vanish beneath a coating of red dirt. Closed his eyes for just a moment and then jolted awake. He had wet his pants. Ray stood up, brushing at the stain on the bathing suit. His checkered suit turned a rusty color as the urine and clay mixed. He was ashamed. Knew Mrs. Burr would be angry. He rubbed the pants until they were dry. The stain wouldn't come off. Ray wished he had something more to wear than his bathing suit and baseball cap.

The black vultures, once circling overhead, were now on the ground and strutting around him. They reminded him of the Rogers' chickens in the trailer. Had the same red eyes and scaly shoes. Their claws and pointed beak frightened Ray, just as the chickens had. He kicked at the birds, but they only sauntered away in a semicircle or flopped a few steps with their awkward wings. They kept looking at him. Ray peered down the road. There was a white line. Butler would find him and take care of these birds.

Ray took off his baseball cap. Examined its embossed letters and the sweatband inside. It was black with perspiration. He knew where first base was. A red ash can. No, the trailer, that's it. He hoped Butler would come soon; he would show him that he knew where first base is and "You're out." He can do that. The gas station had a red oil drum.

The sun dimmed. And shadows moved across the copper-red earth and rolled past him. They reminded him of the animals on the merry-go-round, only these animals slipped flat across the ground and changed shape. Ray put his hat back on and tried to catch a moving shadow with his hand; it went right through him. He tried again. His own shadow was easier to find. It held still. Then, just as he moved, it jumped with him. His stamping foot set off a cloud of dust. "Where is he?" His mind jolted a fearful message. Ray stamped the ground, hoping Butler would hear the thumps. And come up stairs and get angry at him. "I'm here!" Ray cried as loud as he could. "I'm here! I'm here! I have the map like you asked!"

The station operator, hearing the yelling, finally approached Ray. He had been standing in the same place for three nights and two days. The station operator told Ray to walk down the road three miles to a police station and ask for help. He told Ray in the best way he could that he would tell his friend where he had gone. Ray watched the man intently, watched the direction in which he pointed, and saw the three fingers and then the fingers walking. The man scratched a star in the dirt and pointed again. Ray paced back and forth while the station operator left and returned. The operator gave Ray a warm Coca-Cola. When the drink was finished, the gas-station man grinned. He had no teeth. The man with no teeth took Ray by the hand and started walking in the direction he had pointed. Ray kept looking, looking over his shoulder at his standing place—looking for a returning pickup.

The captain in charge of the local jail was on duty by himself when Ray and his escort entered the office. Ray heard what he knew was a baseball game being broadcast over a small radio in the corner of the office. He listened for names: Willie Mays, Juan Marichal, or Bye-bye, baby. The jailer and the man with no teeth were talking, making it difficult for Ray to hear the game. The man with no teeth left with a flurry of "hand talk" and Spanish. He waved to Ray as he walked out onto the roadside. It was getting dark outside.

The officer gave Ray a pair of long pants and a sweater. Then sat him in the corner next to the radio and gave him a dish of Mexican pasta called *sopa fideo*. Ray vomited the food. After the accident, the captain led Ray to the prison yard. There was nothing else to do.

Ray stood like a statue in the prison yard. Then he tried to escape his own stench by moving about. There were families in the yard camping out with imprisoned relatives. Radios blared, curses were tossed into the air, prostitutes lifted their skirts at the potential new customer. Children ran and circled Ray in a game they saved only for the weak and feeble. His smell drove everyone else off.

Ray climbed into the tree in the middle of the jail compound. He clung to the branches, afraid that he had climbed too high and afraid that he would fall into the pit of clamoring people below. The matches. Ray fumbled with the book of matches. Methodically, he pulled each match from the cover and struck it—felt the momentary solace of the light—then winced as the flame died against the night air. One at a time he lighted his shooting stars and watched as they floated and streaked into the void of screaming darkness. Then the cover was empty.

Fear surged within him in an uncontrollable stream. Ray tried to think about baseball and tried to reach into his pocket to find the button. He could do neither. It was as if a basket of snakes had suddenly broken loose in his mind.

Close the door Raymond— Tongues. I can mark my arm. It's in the door. Don't take the pen. Fire. Things are burning. I didn't start the fire. Fourteen Stations of the Cross. Yes, you must kneel. Kneel before Christ. Everyone is crying. The things you do causes Christ his pain. Christ was nailed to the cross because of you. Raymond get your hand out of the fire—you have killed somebody. The floor is cold. Don't close the door. Please don't. Tongues huge tongues are burning. Willie Mays hit—I like Willie Mays their eyes are eaten out. Chickens with no eyes. Locking the door. Candles are fire. Birthday candles burning and hats on the table. My mother crying in the kitchen. Put out the candles. Ice cream. I can put my hand in the flame, for Christ. Ice cream. We had birthday ice cream. I don't like those men they are hurting my arm. John Butler is twisting my arm. The ice cream is melting. I have it in my pocket a button. I didn't mean to keep it. Or put out the candle. Tongues are licking me. I'll burn them. I'm on fire.

The gas station operator was standing next to the captain with the badge. They were talking and sweeping the air with their hands. They coaxed Ray out of the tree.

"The matches, the matchbook here, on the ground, it belongs to you, yes? It says that you are from the trailer park close to Uruapan. Mr. Dias here, he thinks you should take the bus and go to the trailer park at Tingubatu, that's where the gringos with the long hair go. It is where they live." Ray was too frightened to answer. The policeman tapped the match cover and questioned, "Tingubatu, yes? That is where you will find your friend? Surely he will return for you, yes!"

Ray tried to speak, but all he could think of was the empty match cover. He reached forward and took the cover from the officer. "Good, surely your friend will return for you here," the officer repeated hopefully. "It's Tingubatu, on the highway from Uruapan." Both men searched in their pockets for the thirty pesos needed for the bus trip.

The man with no teeth waited with Ray for the bus and told the driver where to let the passenger off. The bus driver must have been a relative of the gas-station operator. He, too, had no front teeth. The operator pressed an extra peso into Ray's hand as he boarded the blue and white bus.

<u>May 3, 1972</u>

The yellow trailer was right where he and Butler had left it. Ray couldn't wait to step inside. See the familiar things. His drawer with the jewel box and Elvis Presley clipping. And the icebox with its supply of bread and beer. Upon opening the door, a dozen eyes darted in his direction. At first, Ray couldn't make out who or what was inside the trailer. His eyes were still adjusting from the bright outdoor light to the indoor shadows. Before he could make the adjustment, Spanish words were flying in his direction, and fingers were poking in the ribs and waving in front of his nose.

Outside the trailer he was surrounded by a Mexican family. The mother and father were both shouting at him and continuing to jab. Ray fell backward as the pair continued to scratch the sky with their fingers. Ray cringed. The man gestured for Ray to go away. He showed money and pointed to the trailer, followed by some chest thumping. The woman was speaking rapidly and pantomiming the selling of the trailer by the blond man, who pushed his hands through his hair like this and took things out of the trailer and put them in his truck, then put them back in the trailer, then back in the truck, and drove off, the truck full of everything in the trailer, drove off that way.

They were still yelling and pointing as Ray pulled himself up and walked away. He could see the wheelless buses and vans in the corner of the trailer park, so he headed in that direction. But, like the yellow trailer, they had become homes for Mexican families. Clotheslines draped with white pants and shirts linked the vehicles and made them into a kind of tent city. The great, colorfully painted buses sat wheelless and rusting—evidence of another lost culture. Star Flower and the children— Speckled Frog, Moonbeam, and Abraham—were gone. Ray wandered throughout the trailer park, listening for some English. Something familiar. Someone to talk to. But no one understood when he asked about the truck and his drawer with the Elvis Presley picture.

Ray found a place to stay in a cement storm drain. The concrete was warm during the day and held some of this heat into the night. If he sat curled in a ball, he could keep his feet from falling in the stagnant water in the bottom of the drain. Ray tried to keep his eyes open. That was the hardest part. Whenever he closed his eyes, he was haunted by his fears. They became real. Began to talk to him. Began to live in the wall of the sewer and the rocks on its floor. Ray fumbled with the reflector button. As long as he could hold on to his button, he was safe. Ray studied the button in the fading light. It reflected part of his face. Ray didn't like what he saw. It was crawling. He tried to pray, but the only image that came to his mind was a burning hand. He swung wildly at the thing crawling on his face. A dragonfly. It took flight. The dragonfly was the most frightening thing. They were all over. Flying all over him. Hundreds of dragonflies touching his mouth and climbing into his ears. Sewing his eyes shut.

Meals Are Not Included

<u>May 30, 1972</u>

"Look at this!" Carver tapped the list in his hand. "He's running, your friend John Henry Butler is on the run." Miss Croce studied the list, she didn't see how it brought on Carver's elation. Or understand how Carver got his information.

"What do you see in this list that I'm missing?" she asked, "and where did you get it, anyway?"

Carver was patient and deliberate, like a cougar about to pounce on its prey. "The list comes from *hard* investigative work." He laughed at his own joke, then went on. "I called some friends in the FBI, and a bank examiner I know helped me with the bank statements—look here!"

5/10 Bad check cashed by Butler with Bank of
America.
5/15 Bad check cashed with UCB.
5/20 Butler went to Busvan and removed the
belongings of the Rogers. Had them shipped to
Mrs. Burr in the name of Richard Turner.
5/27 Butler cashed bad check at Harvey's Club, Reno.
5/28 Butler passed bad check at Grand Auto Parts,
Daly City.

"The Busvan idea was mine. Figured the Rogers might have something in storage—property—and knew our boy would want his hands on it."

Sherry was still a little confused. "So what does all this mean?"

Carver explained. "It's a pattern, most criminals have a pattern, go to the same bars, do a crime the same way—"

"And for Mr. Butler?" Sherry interrupted.

"For our friend, well he made the mistake he's trying to sell the Rogers' goods at his mother's—that's where he'll show up—Mrs. Burr's. And when we find him we find Raymond Martinez. They are either traveling together or Butler's left him someplace."

Sherry smiled. "Well, aren't you going to ask me what I found out, with my four-hundred-thirty-eight-dollar phone bill?"

"Who got billing?" Carver asked.

"Alabama!"

After Carver stopped laughing and slapping his hands in delight, Sherry came in with the clincher. "Okay, Mr. Detective, are you ready for this—it's gonna knock you out of your shoes."

"Come on, come on, what did you find?"

Sherry pulled from her briefcase a letter. "Take a look at this, Mr. Tibbs." Carver gave her his "don't give me that Mr. Tibbs stare! He read the letter.

American Citizens Services Office
CONSULATE GENERAL OF THE
UNITED STATES OF AMERICA

Guadalajara, Jalisco, Mexico

April 24, 1972

Miss Sherry Croce
Department of Social Services
585 Bush Street
San Francisco, California 94102

Re: MARTINEZ, Raymond
03-016-9657

Dear Mr. Croce:

This letter is written upon the request of Mr. John
Butler, guardian for Mr. Raymond Martinez.

Enclosed you will find your letter dated March 22,
requesting our assistance with Mr. Martinez's case.

Specifically to answer your inquiries: (1) Mr.
Martinez is living with Mr. John H. Butler. (2) Mr.
Martinez pays 100 pesos per day for room and board
or about $240 per month. (3) Meals are included in
the above cost.

The address for Mr. Butler or Mr. Martinez is as
follows:
Lista de Correos, Uruapan, Michoacán, Mexico.

I hope this information has been helpful.

Sincerely,

Robert J. Chavez
American Vice-Consul

Encl. As stated

"The department thinks this is 'sufficient cause' to drop the case," Sherry said, "that Ray Martinez is safe and his guardian Mr. Butler is providing satisfactory care."

Carver was furious. "Safe my foot—they just don't want to get off their asses and do a job; call this consular character and ask him one question. Did he actually *see* Martinez, or did he just talk with Butler? Butler can con butter out of a rock. Two to one that consular fellow was busy and signed whatever Butler asked. I mean Butler is your blond blue eyes all-American." Carver couldn't wait. He picked up the telephone. "Give me the charge number you're using—"

Later, the call complete, he hung up the receiver with a soft click. "The guy never saw Martinez. Said Butler was a businessman interested in investing in Mexico. I think we better find this Butler fast."

Carver sat back for a second, scanning the list in front of him and the letter. He had an idea. "Umm, I want you to call this consular fellow back in about an hour—tell him you are a friend of Raymond Martinez and Mr. Martinez has inherited a fortune and must be found immediately. That interested parties in this case are going to the Department of State and Congress over the disappearance and complicity in that disappearance by a consular office. That should kick some dirt loose."

Sherry balked at this suggestion. "But who's going to contact the State Department and—"

"I am!" Carver replied with a confident grin.

Maliche Mariana The Crying Lady

May 31, 1972

Dogs bark in the trailer camp. Ray Martinez scrapes the inside of an overturned garbage can and throws a rock at the marauders. The salty crust of the can tastes good. His mouth waters at the touch of any food.

This is the first stop on Ray's daily circuit. Each garbage can is inspected for any scrap of meat, spoiled fruit, or container that might hold a drop of food. Tea that is thrown away can be gathered and licked. Fruit and vegetable peelings can be chewed. The dogs compete for these tasty morsels. They must be shoved away with a stick or rock.

The next stop on Ray's round is the bathhouse in the center of the trailer camp. Here Ray takes off his clothes and bathes, with one hand splashing water on his sores and blisters. His feet need the most care. Ray lost his shoes. Or else someone took them. His feet have gradually hardened. Now only a few blisters contain a milky puss. And Ray has found that washing and drying his feet with the husk of a tortilla makes his feet feel better.

After his bath, Ray likes to go to the edge of the park where the women do washing. This washing water comes out of a single faucet that is far from the septic tank seepage at the bath house. So the water is cleaner here than in the bathhouse. The women soak the clothing in tubs, then wring it out and beat it against the flat rocks that surround the fountain. Children play within eyesight of their parents. They love to run and kick a ball.

And they let Ray join in. He plays baseball. Runs to real or imaginary bases. The children are playing football and tag. It doesn't matter. Everyone has fun.

The children call Ray Maliche Mariana. It's a woman's name—the Crying Lady. But he carries a fate similar to a real Maliche Mariana, whose name was Llorana. She was an Indian woman who translated for Cortés and guided him to the Aztec capital. Then bore his child. Seeing the child was part white, she killed it and now lives in eternal grief. She is without a homeland, like this Raymond Martinez, who befriended the gringo Butler and then was left to eat out of garbage cans and cry in the night.

In the afternoon, when the breath of the middle day began to move the sun, Ray climbed to his secret place. It was a large mound of rocks on a plateau above the trailer camp, the old Aztec pyramid used by the hippies for their celebrations. Here it was quiet, and here he could talk to himself. Mostly this talk was of baseball and Elvis. Ray still couldn't remember how many home runs Willie Mays hit, but he was getting close. He would talk out loud, giving pieces of the puzzle to the wind—hoping somehow the missing numbers would somehow fall in place. He repeated this ritual each day—sitting facing the pile of rocks and speaking in a deliberate voice, telling the rocks. "Willie Mays hit . . . home runs. Willie Mays hit . . . home runs. Willie Mays hit . . . against Cincinnati. Willie Mays hit . . . against Cincinnati, home runs against Cincinnati. The rocks never answered. But sitting and telling them, well, it felt good.

After that came his most special moment. The moment he most looked forward to every day. In a practiced and stylized routine, Ray slowly stood and faced the valley below. Then, with great bravado, he took an imaginary guitar into his hands and began to move his fingers across its neck and through its heart. With his WHIZ once more in his hands, he was once again standing on the truck in front of all those people. He was Elvis Presley.

Ray closed his eyes. Rotated his hips. And sang as wildly as he could. Jumping over the rocks, yelling at the sun.

> *One, two, three, o'clock*
> *Four o'clock Rock!*
> *Five, six, seven o'clock*
> *Eight o'clock Rock!*
> *Nine, ten, eleven o'clock*
> *Twelve o'clock Rock!*
> *We're gonna Rock around*
> *The clock tonight.*
> *We're gonna Rock Rock Rock*
> *Rock Rock Rock*
> *We're gonna Rock Rock Rock*
> *Rock Rock Rock*
> *We're gonna Rock*
> *Around the clock tonight.*
> *We're gonna . . .*

It was on one of these days at this time of day that he saw Tonalpoulqui, the fortune-teller. She, too, liked this place of memories. And became an audience for this singer of songs. For days she just listened to the chant, then picked her way through the lava rocks and out of sight. But one day, while she slowly collected sticks for her fire, Ray mimed her every movement. That began their dance. A minuet. Yards, years, and cultures apart. She stooping down. Ray bending earthward. She placing a stick in her bundle. Ray duplicating the movement. She revolving slowly in the light. Ray revolving slowly in the light. Catching a trace of her smile. She and Ray pointing to the rocks. This silent mime went on day after day. Closer and closer. Until they were a touch apart. She dabbed her lips with thin, frail fingers. Ray placed his hand over his mouth. She removed his hand and spoke.

She spoke for hours in phrases and lyrics that seemed to hum like the bird and fall like water. He was pleased. He returned the favor. Ray stepped back and took a classic Elvis pose. In full throat he sang out "Jail House Rock." His friend smiled. Learned the words. And sang along.

> *Let's Rock*
> *Everybody Let's Rock*
> *Everybody in the Whole Cell Block*
> *Was dancing to the Jail House Rock.*
>
> *Number 47 said to Number 3*
> *You're the cutest jailbird I ever did see*
> *I sure would be delighted by your company*
> *Come on and do the Jail House Rock with me.*
> *Let's Rock . . .*

Afterward the old woman with a face of parchment promised Ray the meaning of the rock and sky and the duty of the human being. But in exchange for these she asked a price—would Ray kiss her? Ray didn't hesitate—he saw her eyes and the soft sandpapered tips of her fingers. He reached out for her and kissed her. It was a gentle kiss. The woman smiled. No teeth! Raymond laughed.

And so Tonalpoulqui spoke, and Ray listened. "If you dry the flesh of a hummingbird until it is powder and put it into the drink of a woman, she will see only you . . ." Every day they met in their place and talked. Ray tried to explain the *Brady Bunch* and television. Tonalpoulqui tried to answer with the obligation of Aztec parents toward their children.

> They would begin to teach them:
> how they should live,
> how they should respect others,
> how they were to dedicate themselves to
> what was good and righteous;
> how they were to avoid evil,
> fleeing unrighteousness with strength,
> refraining from perversion and greed.

> She spoke for days.

The father, his heart is good,
he is careful of things;
he is compassionate, he is concerned,
he is the foresight, he is support,
he protects with his hands.
He places before them a large mirror,
a mirror pierced on both sides;
he is a large torch that does not smoke . . .

When Ray tried to ask the most important question
of all—Tonalpoulqui primped herself, licked her hands
like a cat cleaning its paws—wetted the ends of her
braided hair—lit a cigar, and puffed it violently to fend
off evil spirits. But before he had a chance to say it
clearly, she was speaking of this place and the eagles that
fly here, eagles that were men, the crowns of feathers
eagle men wore as they dove from the pole tower, the
digging of the hole, and ceremonial tasks . . .

Throughout her chant Ray sat politely repeating his
own question in his head. He kept whispering it to himself. When she became silent, he said it out loud. "The
most important question, question I want to ask, the
most important question is how many home runs, Willie
Mays hit how many home runs against Cincinnati?"

Tonalpoulqui didn't budge or remove her concentration from the pile of rocks. Ray said it again. And
Tonalpoulqui answered, "Willie, Willie Mays, you must
tell me the day and hour of his birth, there is the answer,
on the day he was born. . . ."

Each day Ray would leave this place of rocks and
cross in the twilight to his home in the culvert. This was
the hardest time of his life. He was always hungry. And
now alone. He could see other families enjoying this
time of fading light, often sitting out in front of their trail-
ers, drinking and smoking. In his shadowy course to the
culvert he wished for the company of the yellow trailer
and Butler and Mr. and Mrs. Rogers, even Mrs. Burr.
He often thought of ice cream and chocolate and beer.
His nightly trek to the culvert didn't allow for any con-

tact with the trailer-park residents. Raymond was afraid of being screamed at, and the chickens and dogs became nighttime beasts.

So each night he scurried to his cement cave. Each night he inspected his things. The ribbon from the thistle bush. And most valued of all—the reflector button from his guitar. Just holding the button made him feel better. Each night he looked for the map, but like his shoes, it had found another home. Ray worried about the map. And what Butler would say when he didn't have it. Each night he repeated the frantic search for the map.

There were some new things Raymond had acquired. A coffee can with a wire handle was used to hold water. Each night he dipped the can into the seepage in the bottom of the cement casing. Then mixed food scraps he saved from scrounging in the garbage cans with leaves and a handful of dirt. He boiled this concoction as his evening meal. Ray was good at making a fire. He had found a box of matches. There were four matches left in the box.

You Can't Be Lost If You Don't Know Where You're Going

June 3, 1972
Ray gradually took his place in the universe of the camp. He was welcomed to the birth of an Indian child. Watched as its placenta was buried: "Man is a plant that grows and branches and flowers on earth." Listened to the poetry that was recited to the newborn. Was awed when Tonalpoulqui, the fortuneteller, measured the hour of birth against the tides of the planets and stars. Waited with others for the fortuitous day to arrive when the child would be named. Learned to sing the song of life.

> The gold and black butterfly
> Is sipping the nectar
> The flower bursts into bloom:
> Ah, my friends, it is my heart.
> I send down a shower of
> white frangipani flowers.

And later, Tonalpoulqui showed Ray how to prepare for death. "See the oldest women there, see what they wear, the simplest adornments: a single red thread, like a vein of blood, woven into their garments. It is a sign of coming death. If at death one owns possessions that require labor from others, the dead person must work to pay for those in the next world. The simple blouse with the thread of red needs less labor in the afterlife." As Tonalpoulqui spoke, Ray noticed her blouse with the single thread of red.

June 14, 1972

When Tonalpoulqui entered *miccatzintle*—the state
of death—Ray was asked to stand by her side and softly
sing his songs. She lay on a table surrounded by candles
and offerings to take on her journey: food, drink, twelve
black beans, twelve kernels of corn—all to assure that
her afterlife would be filled with work. Ray was surprised
at how small Tonalpoulqui looked. And how content.
Her death mask was already looking upon the other
world.

Ray sang songs no one but Tonalpoulqui could understand. He sang them slowly and respectfully, as was
his duty. Upon finishing his songs he placed a ribbon, his
pink ribbon, at the side of this old woman who had asked
him for a kiss. He bent down and kissed her one more
time, for the long journey. This Tonalpoulqui, this old
woman with skin like the earth, this friend.

When Ray finished, one of the men held out to Ray
a cupful of pulque—"a drink to bring gladness." The
man said Tonalpoulqui had told him of *pulque*. It was
made from the maguey cactus, and only Aztecs of ad-
vanced age were allowed to drink it. Or someone about
to die. Or be sacrificed. For a moment Ray was afraid he
was going to have his heart torn out. But then all the
other men were drinking. And all the men can't be pre-
paring to die. Although they did all fall down on the
ground.

Everything was as Tonalpoulqui said it would be.
The men put on leather masks of the jaguar and fought to
bring rain. And food once again tasted good in his
mouth. He walked about, and people of the trailer camp
offered him a place at their table. He sang his songs,
giving pleasure to those that heard his words. She
laughed—Ray remembered the laugh, it was her joke—
she told the people of the trailer park that "the crying
man" was of the Chichimecs,
             of the Toltecs,
                of the Acolhuas,
                   of the Tecpanecs,

and she laughed. It was their joke. He asked about Willie Mays, and she answered Toltecs don't ask that question. Ray missed this lady with no teeth. She had been kind and was a friend.

Without Tonalpoulqui, loneliness became Ray's companion and tormentor. At the place of rocks, he tried to sing, but there was no one to listen.

No Tonalpoulqui to put his arms around. No longer the pleasure of the touch of her hand. No one to be quiet with. Drink with. No one to tease or laugh with. No one to work with. No one to wait for, surprise, or need. He threw rocks to the air, hoping for a response. There was no sound. No cry.

Ray visited the place of rocks daily, hoping Tonalpoulqui would reappear from the rocks, as she had the first time they met. This pyramid of rock and dome of shrub brush became Ray's sanctuary. From this pinnacle he sat with his legs folded under him and followed the path of the sun. Slowly, like a plant deprived of water and light, he felt himself being sucked into the earth.

In this state of despair Ray's mind began its chant of destruction. Surely he had done something bad. Something terrible. The church door opened, drawing his eye to the altar. Angels peered at him from the ceiling. And Jesus looked down upon him from the cross. Ray gathered twigs from the top of the earthen mound and placed them into a tight pile. Then carefully added branches of pine and madrone. The evening sky was tinted purple as Raymond lit the pyre. Flames cracked and jumped into the night. Sparks swirled in the turbulent winds ascending the face of the pyramid. Ray felt the hot blast against his entire body. As if in an ancient prayer, Ray raised his arms—the palm of each hand facing the blaze.

For a long time Ray stood that way. Even after the fire had become bright embers. Ray still stood facing the furnace—palms upraised, waiting. . . .

John Henry Butler waved at him from the driver's seat of the pickup. Asked him to get a map. Ray handed the map to Butler, and John Henry just laughed. "You can't be lost," he said—as he'd said so many times before—"if you don't know where you're going!" Butler used to laugh every time he said that. Every time the truck was out of gas or the Rogers had wandered off. The same joke— "You can't be lost if you don't know where you're going." And he'd laugh.

Ray and Butler were at the graveyard, looking up at the words in the chapel. *Muertos*. Ray knew what the word meant—the dead. Ray knew all the words, and Butler didn't! ESPERAMOS LA RESURECCIÓN DE LOS MUERTOS—we hope for the resurrection of the dead. Ray knows things like other people. Butler is wrong. You're lost if you don't know where home is. Ray was sure of it. You have to have a home. And he had a home. He knew where it was—with Mrs. Burr and the Rogers. And walking down Haight Street, getting a doughnut for Jake and swinging in the park, listening to the Giants with Larry. That was his home. That's where he belonged. Where he had to get.

The fire was dying. Embers exploded in one last gorging of oxygen and then curled inward. Tears filled Ray's eyes. And his heart beat faster. Home. Home. That one idea flooded every emotion and every thought. In a burst of joy Ray turned from the dying fire and shouted at the top of his lungs, "Anyone here know Willie Mays?" The silence confirmed Ray's judgment: Here is totally alone. Nothing around him can hear his voice. Nothing here can know his hurt or respond to his needs. Ray felt a tingling surge of confidence. Of jubilation. A knowing that was new and exciting. Ray's hands trembled. Tears rolled down his cheeks. Ray was sobbing when he cuffed both hands around his mouth like a bullhorn and yelled a final yell. "Thank you for everything but I'm leaving now—good-bye good-bye now. I'm going home."

I Hate Cows

June 4, 1972
The eyelid of morning was about to lift. Ray circled
the garbage cans one last time, then headed for the
bathhouse. He washed quickly and inspected his pants
pocket. Everything of value was stuffed there—a twisted
wire coat hanger, two matches, and the reflector. Ray
took out the button and looked at it like a jeweler view-
ing the faces of a splendid stone. The veins of plastic
reflected the first rays of light. Ray stuffed his treasure
into his pocket and started the journey home.

Only one road carved its way from the trailer park to
intersect with the highway, and it had existed for cen-
turies. It was part of the Aztec road system—a single
lane of flat stone, with the center line of stone turned
edgewise—maybe a predecessor of the white line but
more likely a mark of craftsmanship. Like all Aztec art, it
was unsigned. The artist, architect, and builder unknown. Ray followed the cobblestones. He was so intent
on stepping only on the center stones that he was unaware that the trailer-park folk had joined him. They
stayed behind him at a respectable distance.

The bedraggled procession clanked its way for a mile or so before a small child broke ranks and tried to catch Ray's attention. First she brushed his arm, then in frustration tugged on his hand. When he at last noticed her, the child forced a round loaf of bread into Ray's hand, then scurried back into the crowd. As Ray turned to thank her, someone else approached from his other side and repeated the child's gesture—first gently touching Ray's arm, then delivering a gift of food. Ray's hands were juggling tomatoes and a loaf of bread when he pivoted in embarrassment and tried to march on.

Next an older man came forward, touched Ray's arm, and placed the handles of a straw satchel around his wrist. Again, when Ray tried to thank the gift giver, the man simply withdrew into the ranks of the now-smiling faces. Ray put his tomatoes and bread into the straw basket and once again tried to act as if he knew what he was doing—where he was going. He turned and told them they could go with him if they wanted. He was going to Haight Street in San Francisco to see his friend Jake.

Then another child placed a container of maize called *tlacatlaolli* into his sack. And another child crowded forward to present a handful of amaronth seeds. An older woman proudly presented a glass jar of *huauhtli*, a soup made of fat *frijoles*.

By the time he reached the lip of the highway, Ray's packet was filled with foodstuff and good-luck amulets. A broad band of concrete greeted him. It seemed like a river of asphalt connecting the great mountains to the north and to the south. The highway presented Ray with his first challenge. He had to decide which way to go on it. A huge canvas-backed truck came screaming down the highway. Its windshield was fringed with lace, and a golden cross dangled from the rearview mirror. Cezar Ali was spelled in chrome across the grille. After the truck blasted past, its eagle mud flaps flapped a salute. Ray confidently followed the truck. When he looked over his shoulder for the approval of his friends, he saw they were slowly retreating down the ancient road.

The pavement was cool. And walking in the morn-

ing air seemed easy. Raymond had a plan. He would
walk as far as he could and at the same time keep sight of
his pyramid. It was only a green bump in a sea of hills,
but the way it was level at the top made it stand out. All
the other mountains were cones. Ray was quite pleased
with his plan—just keep walking and keep looking at the
pyramid. As long as he could see the top of Tingubatu he
was safe.

Buses and trucks owned the highway. They roared
past with little regard for curves and occasional lost cows.
They could be heard coming for miles; and when they
blasted past, they sent waves of dust curling into the air.
He was glad when these monsters and their noxious trail
of fumes passed and he could enjoy the countryside
again. The delicate ticking of insects and flight of snowlike seeds. The pine forests next to the highway gave a
gentle coolness to the air and the scent of Christmas.
Lakes of corn filled the openings in the forest, while the
distant volcanoes stood like purple ice cream cones.

As Ray walked, he often checked the flat pyramid
behind him. It was strange, he thought, how small this
place of rocks was looking. And how it would momentarily disappear in a turn of the roadway. He found himself walking slower when the pyramid was in sight and
almost running when his stone lighthouse disappeared.

A flight of chattering birds directed Ray's eyes to the
side of the highway. They swooped and danced around a
dark swollen form. At first, Ray couldn't decipher what
he was seeing. Then he realized it was a decapitated cow.
Hoofed legs pointed at Ray like huge fingers. Above the
cow, a silver cross stuck precariously in the embankment.

Ray tried to make sense of what he was seeing. The
cow—it must have been hit by a truck. But the cross—
why is it uprooted and tilting to one side? What is it
doing here so far from people? Who has tended it? Left a
straw wreath and rusted coffee can? Ray climbed the embankment above the cow and touched the cross. His
hand recoiled. It was made of bone covered by aluminum foil and was strangely cold. Ray quickly followed his
instinct. He piled rocks around the base of the cross so it

would stand upright. Then he stood back and examined his work. He felt good that the cross was upright, but he hated the smell and the sight of the dead cow.

Back on the highway, Ray could no longer see his pyramid. It was no longer just temporarily screened by branches or hiding behind a turn in the road—this time Ray felt he was looking toward the right place, but the marker was just not there. Ray clambered faster up the highway to get to a clearing or higher vantage point. Without success. Finally, he was running. He ran until his breath was dry and his feet were bleeding. Then collapsed in a heap on a gravel spit. He felt weak and hungry. He reached for the satchel of food and drink. It was gone! Ray searched his pockets and traced his body with one hand. It was gone! He frantically dug at the dirt and gravel. Jumped around like a magician looking for a wayward illusion. It was gone. He must have put it down when he fixed that cross. It was that cow's fault. If he hadn't fixed that cross. It was that cow's fault. If he hadn't stopped to look at the cow—that damn cow! That damn cow made me stop. I hate cows—it was that cow's fault. A truck rumbled past and drowned Ray's loud curses. Then a bus. Then it was strangely silent. Ray's body shook. He couldn't see his mountain, and he had lost the gift of food. And he was thirsty. And what to do now?

Ray circled the gravel spit and angrily kicked loose stones. He didn't want to go back. He had started. He didn't want to stop. And if he couldn't see the place of rocks, then he would have to think of another way to get where he was going. Ray decided to count his steps. He had seen signs with numbers, so that's it, he'd count. Counting must mean something. So he took a step and counted. "I hate damn dead cows—one." Then another—"two."

One, two, three, four . . . Ray could count to ten. He stepped and counted. The rhythm of counting made him feel better, stronger. He was getting someplace. One, two, three. . . . A giddy feeling overwhelmed him. He reached into his pocket and felt the reflector bounce in his hand with each stride. He knew he was smiling, laughing at himself. And the idea of being home. Ray's steps became a swagger, and his counting became a song. At first, Ray was humming and then singing. Singing to the cows with heads. And the noisy trucks. The eggshell volcanoes.

> *One for the money*
> *Two for the show*
> *Three to get ready*
> *Now go cat go*
> *But don't you . . .*

Ray stopped suddenly as if he had been shot. A terrible thought shuddered through his body and out his lips. "I hate cows—damn cows!"

Ray slowly continued up the road, sometimes singing about blue suede shoes and sometimes pausing to curse a dead cow.

His Shadow Crossed The Earth

June 6, 1972

"Damn cow, I hate that cow!" Ray strutted down the roadway, cursing. At times, he pretended to have the basket swinging on his arm. He would pause and open it and help himself to a make-believe apple. Unscrew the top from a bottle and tilt its contents into his mouth. Roll his tongue over his lips in mock appreciation.

Ray then would laugh and offer his friends the birds a piece of bread. Then he'd realize he was kidding himself and he had nothing but an empty hand to offer. Stepping in and out of this imaginary world, Ray tore pieces of bread and scattered them along the trail. The birds swooped down and pecked at the barren soil. Then, as if to continue the game, took flight and thanked Ray by fluttering their wings in excitement. With great fanfare, Ray tucked his missing gifts into his nonexistent basket and continued on his way.

For days Ray walked with the constant roar of the trucks and with his shadow. Then, one morning, his shadow was missing. Ray tried walking slower, still no shadow. Then running. No shadow. Ray began walking in a tight circle, waiting for the shadow to catch up. His shadow had run away. Now, because he had lost his shadow, Ray feared he had died.

Ray put his hand on the roadway, then lifted it slightly. There was no hint of a shadow. Ray put his hand back on the dusty roadbed and with his other hand traced the shape of his fingers and thumb. Removing his hand, Ray saw the pattern of his hand in the dust. Though it wasn't a shadow, it was proof he was alive. Ray wriggled his fingers in front of his nose.

Behind his flickering fingers dark clouds billowed and draped above him. The dark coolness brushed his face. A hushed silence. Air thickened. It was like entering church. The sky teased his eye. Closed over Ray like a vaulted ceiling. Ray heard a door slamming.

Huge raindrops plopped on the ground with a cushioned thud. Each black pearl quivered for a second, then flattened. More drops fell. They collided in destructive bursts and set off a rhythmic clapping. The door slammed again. Lightning splintered the clouds and torched into a volcano. Water spilled from the cracked sky.

Ray was mesmerized. He stood perfectly still and stretched out both his arms. He didn't know what to ask or say. He could only stand like Jesus on the cross. Surely that was the right thing to do—in church—in the rain—stand like Jesus.

The cold rain pelting the heated highway turned to steam. Rain was falling to the earth and racing skyward at the same time. Ray stood transfixed in this cloud chamber. Stood with his arms outstretched.

The torrent slowed. Great drops tumbled from the

moving pine branches. Steam continued to rise from the ground. Ray felt that his arms were being moved up and down by this gentle current. He felt he could fly in this wonderful mist. Distant thunder slammed. Ray didn't care. Ray stroked the wet air with his arms. Then waved his arms as if to take flight—looked down to see if his feet were leaving the ground. He saw something else. His shadow crossed the earth.

Images Fell Like Confetti

July 1, 1972

Ray had walked for days, but this was the first city in his path. Though he didn't know it, he had returned to Uruapan, the city where he and Butler shared dreams of robbing a bank and starting a "jitney." There were so many people. Moving so quickly. So many distractions. Walking on the highway, Ray had only to contend with passing trucks and the villages that clung to its edge. Cows without heads. For the most part, Ray's journey had been foot in front of foot. This was something he could do. His mind had chased ghosts, but his feet had only one path to follow. Now that path broke up into a maze of cross streets.

The city smothered all the comforts that Ray enjoyed on the road. The sky, with its trail of light, was blotted out by the city's misty aura. The cool breeze that sifted down the valleys was replaced by the foul breath of buses. The eye that had looked inward was yanked outward. Pleasing aromas of manure, wet grass, and pine were replaced by odors of boot polish, cheap perfume, and spoiling vegetables.

Everything in Uruapan revolved around its central plaza. Cars, trucks, and buses circled it before swirling off to their destination. A procession of young girls in long white dresses clogged the street, trapping buses against the curb. A priest carrying a ceramic Virgin Mary on his head led the tide of white and brown, young and old. And a small Volkswagen with a loudspeaker mounted on its roof nosed its way into the rear of the parade—blaring the songs of the Madonna. Everyone seemed to be singing the chant. Merchants and shoppers stopped their business to crowd to the edge of the street and join in the song.

An ambulance wound its siren into the air. Like a parting sea, elders pulled their white angels out of its way. The ambulance rolled down the center of the street, its siren blasting. The Volkswagen loudspeaker encouraged the river of marchers to sing louder. Trucks and buses followed in the ambulance's wake and forced the priest and his angels to walk on the sidewalk. They filled the narrow passage with their metronome chant until they filed into the church on the corner of the plaza. Its great doors closed with a slam. Silken banners fluttered from nails driven into the ancient doors. Ray picked out words *basta, muerta, comunista*.

Outside the church the afternoon was turning to night. Buildings with faces of lime, rose, and peach turned a smoky purple. Merchants and customers began to return to their private pleasures. Some peddlers still sat with their goods spread before them in a handkerchief—lipstick, plastic plates, pins, combs, toothpaste, toys of all kinds clamored for the eyes' attention. Comic-book stands stood on the sidewalk with the colorful promises of voluptuous women, superheroes, and Donald Duck. Sheets of blue-tinted national lottery tickets and religious calendars fluttered like flags.

The sound of Italian opera swelled into Ray's ear. Spinning to one side of the street, Ray saw a coffin. No, coffins. Wooden coffins. Lying on the sidewalk, lounging against the shop wall. Their pine mouths gaping open. Singing Italian!

Ray stumbled in a trance toward the singing boxes. He liked the soaring sound. It was warm and sparked memories of San Francisco's North Beach. Men with cantaloupe faces sitting in the sun. Drinking red wine. Talking of shortstops and center fielders.

Moving closer to the coffins, Ray discovered the source of the music. Sitting on the curb was a red and gold record player. An old man sat next to the music box. With one hand, he cranked the Victrola. With the other, he opened and closed the lid of the closest casket. Ray smiled. The man was making the box move. The coffins were not singing. Still, it was funny, and as the old man knew, it drew a crowd.

When the old man gestured for Ray to try out the coffin, Ray obliged. He lay down in the long box. It felt good to be hugged by the wooden sides. To smell and touch the bleeding globs of resin. Sense the street noise fade into silence as the lid of the box closed above him. Then darkness. A momentary rest. A chance to hear his own breathing. To close his eyes.

A banging noise caused Ray to jolt upward and crack his head against the lid. He forgot where he was. Had he slept? And why was it dark? Someone was holding him down. The lid sprang open, and with it Ray sat upright. The old man smiled. The crowd of evening shoppers stepped back in fear and awe. It was a miracle! Ray laughed and rolled his eyes backward. Then, like in a Frankenstein movie, he stretched both hands outward and moaned. The crowd gasped. People pushed forward. The old man smiled wider, cranked the machine harder, and made a sweep of his hand toward his wonderful coffins.

Ray set off again through the labyrinthine city.

Ray felt himself drifting in and out of consciousness. Time blurred. Night turned to day turned to night. Streets seemed to suddenly tilt skyward or spill downward. Details faded. Ray realized he was walking in a circle. For how long, he couldn't tell. When he had eaten last, he couldn't remember. He knew he had to get something to eat soon, or he would not wake from one of his sleeping bouts.

Ray's only familiar comfort in the alien, baffling city was the movie theater and its poster of James Bond. James Bond reminded Ray of home. He stood in front of the theater, and for a moment he was on Haight Street, waiting for the show. Saturday matinee. And the Giants. Elvis Presley. Ray wondered if this was as close as he would ever get to San Francisco. And his friends. The Beckets and Children's Playground. Then Ray had an idea. A wonderful idea! Ray looked at the theater. People were leaving. Of course! How easy, a way to eat, and eat regularly. Ray smiled and ticked the side of his head to signify great thinking.

Ray watched as people flooded from the theater into the night air. Then he staggered against the flow. Children slid by him. Older people gave him room to pass. Ray squeezed his way inside. It was now empty. He stood quietly in front of the silver screen. The theater air was heavy with the odor of cigarette smoke and the sweet scent of popcorn. Ray giggled, pleased. He could feed himself.

Ray got on his hands and knees and crawled down an empty row of chairs. He wormed along the floor, hungrily scooping sticky globs of candy and pieces of popcorn into his mouth. Having snaked the length of several rows, Ray stopped and sprawled face down against a wad of bubble gum. His pulse throbbed, and his chest hurt. He felt sick. But couldn't stop eating. Ray squirmed the length of the entire room, gorging on popcorn and unfinished Coca-Cola before he was noticed.

The theater manager had followed Ray's progress down the row with some suspicion and worry. Could it be a huge rat? The manager hollered in Spanish. "Rat, rat, get out, this is not your place, it's mine!" Ray bumped his head on the aisle chair and then tangled himself in a sticky mess before straightening up to meet the person whose voice had broken into Ray's meal. Ray stood up, still popping into his mouth pieces of popcorn that had clung to his clothing. "Oh, señor," the manager spoke in animated Spanish. "Get Out! You must get out, this is not your place, it's mine!"

Ray motioned to his mouth. He tried to smile, but when he opened his mouth, all that showed was a glob of half-eaten popcorn and melted Jujyfruits. The chewing gum that Ray had crawled through now clung to him like a pink spider web. That did it! The manager had seen too many horror films. "Get Out! Get Out!" he screamed, his arms flailing wildly. Ray tried desperately to swallow. His gulping noises only served to heighten the manager's terror. He rushed to the lobby of the theater. Ray followed in a slow loping gait. Chewing with each gallop. Tugging at the threads of gum.

In the lobby Ray was confronted by the manager and his mini-skirted ticket taker. The manager shouted something to the girl, and she scampered out of the theater. Ray once again tried to speak, but his words froze. The manager yelling and frantically waving a broom over his head. The old man gestured for Ray to leave. Then swung the broom downward. Its spines scratched across Ray's face. Ray didn't know what to do. To run. Grab the broom from the old man. Or wait. The manager was now frantic. His assailant wouldn't move. He hit Ray again and again. Swinging the broom like a bat, he battered Ray in the stomach. And in the throat.

Ray doubled over, then bolted upright. Nausea surged up through him. His body wrenched in a seizure that spewed vomit into the air. Waving the broom over his head, the manager backed up in disgust. Then aimed the broom handle at Ray's head.

From the pit of his soul Ray let out a yell. Its piercing cry scared both men. With the broom hanging over his head like a guillotine, Ray screamed, "Stop hitting me! Stop hitting me, or I'll kill you!"

Ray had never spoken in his own defense. Or felt rage toward another person. Or even been angry. Now this. This shivering hatred. "Stop hitting me!" There was wonderment mixed with desperate hunger and physical pain. The wonderment of actually talking back. Not hiding. Not accepting abuse. Not pretending.

The manager cleavered the broomstick down on

Ray's head. The stick cracked and splintered. Ray reached above his head, grabbed the broken broom handle, and charged the now-quivering old man. Hovering above him, Ray shouted, "Old man, stop hitting me!" The manager crawled into a corner, with Ray following and standing above him. "Old man, stop hitting me!" Ray repeated. The old man shook his head in agreement.

Then Ray dropped the broken broom handle and dashed into the plaza. His head streamed blood, and he felt he would pass out.

Ray tried desperately to pay attention to what he was seeing. To find some road, some way, out of this place and get back to San Francisco. He propped his eyes open with his fingers, fearing that if they shut he would never see again. He would surely die.

The plaza was alive with people. It was like a merry-go-round. Only this was *not* the carousel that Ray yearned to see. There was no winking lion. And the people on these benches did not wear glow knit caps. Feed the pigeons like Mrs. Rogers. Or listen to the Giants. And there was no Jake. Ray wanted to tell his joke to Jake and give him a doughnut. But everything in this place was strange. Words clattered like small-arms fire. Walls painted with slogans that made no sense. No one to talk to. Or walk to the laundromat with. He couldn't visit Letty and sweep the street for her or be the parade reindeer.

Ray stared at the plaza of Uruapan. Only instead of seeing the old couples and children at play, he saw swirling colored lights like in his room—Mrs. Burr riding an orange shantung sofa, eating a candy cane. Elvis Presley waved and turned his back. The carousel was a pink birthday cake. Ray began a slow stoic walk away from the lighted park. He wasn't sure where he was going. Or why. He retreated to the comfort of memories.

Mother said they were just late. I put the candles on all by myself. Mother helped a little. She said they were just late. Mother made a pink cake. She was beautiful. Pink cake with white frosting. "Don't touch. Don't touch the cake Raymond," that's what she said. It's a birthday cake for Raymond. I put the candles on the top. Nine candles.

Willie Mays was going to come to my birthday party. Willie Mays hit . . . home runs. Mother let me set the table and look out the window. I watched the cars. Friends were going to come to my house from school and little Sam from next door. They were all coming to my party. I talked to Willie Mays on the radio. I watched out the window. Little Sam said Willie Mays can't come to my birthday.

Mother said they were just late. I put the party hats at each place. She let me wear a red hat. Count the days that's all I wanted to do with the pen. Letty gave me the pen. It was new, didn't work too good, though. Mother wrote names on the hats. Little Sam had a red hat, a red hat like mine. His name was on it. I watched out the window till I had to go to the bathroom. Mother made me wear my new pants with suspenders. I couldn't get off the suspenders. Mother walked around the table. Everything was pretty, the colored paper and hats and little baskets of candy. Mother was crying, crying behind the refrigerator door.

She said people would come next year. We would have a party for just the two of us. Mother put on a blue hat. I helped her put away the plates. The candy went into a big cereal bowl. I got a piece. She put the party hats in the trash bag under the sink. We lit all the candles and Mother held me but she couldn't sing happy birthday. It was all right. She died. It's all right. That she couldn't sing happy birthday.

Ray traced detail after detail. As he pushed harder and harder, the events became bright with color and then began to change. Became different. Became more than pictures. Spiral thoughts moving like a corkscrew broke the layers of memory and moved images into the realm of understanding.

No one knows where I keep my Elvis Presley photograph. In the back of the drawer. That's right. Way in the back where no one can find it. And the pen it goes up front, right here! Letty gave me the pen. She said for my birthday. Counting the days until my birthday party that's all I wanted to do. And show Mrs. Burr that I could be good. I did it by marks with the pen, right here. She took the pen away but it belongs in the front of the drawer so it makes noise rolling back and forth. It was my birthday present, the pen.

Ray had lived a life without cause and effect. He'd felt the bombardment of events but never perceived that someone named Raymond might consciously cause something to happen. That was now beginning to change. Change when he stood before the fire he'd made on the place of rocks. Change when he said good-bye and walked away from the trailer camp. Change when he'd wrenched the broom handle from the theater manager. Now even his memories were changing. In every respect, this journey was far more frightening and dangerous.

The pen belongs right in front of the drawer so I can see it and it will roll around. I like that noise. It's like singing happy birthday—happy birthday dear Raymond happy birthday to me. Rolling back and forth. Mrs. Burr doesn't like noise. Turn down that radio she says. I'm going to count to three. She opened the door and took my pen and radio. The radio, I didn't have it on.

She shouldn't have taken my pen and Larry's radio. Larry's radio wasn't on. I was playing and singing. No one sang happy birthday to me, happy birthday to me. Mrs. Burr doesn't like noise, that's what she says, turn down that radio. It's all right, Willie Mays wasn't on the radio, I told her that. She doesn't like noise!

God Is A Dentist

On Sunday morning, Ray Martinez walked into the National Park of Uruapan. At first, just for a second, Ray thought he had entered San Francisco's Golden Gate Park. The same great palms and ferns. And the tea-room pagodas perched above the tropical forest were like those in the Japanese Tea Garden. But then he saw the difference: Here it was incredibly *watery*. The pathways were great flat stones with streamlets gliding between each step. And moisture oozed down the green slate side of volcanic walls. Water shot from the mouths of Tonalpoulqui's gods. And the river Cupatitzio gorged its way through the heart of the park.

In a sunny corner of the park Ray found a playground with swings. He sat in a web seat. It felt good to sway back and forth. Listen to the clank of the chain. That familiar noise from those hours in San Francisco's Children's Playground. Clank. Clank. Clank. The park was filling with families coming from church—men in their dark slacks and loose white shirts; women in straight skirts and raven-winged shawls. Children skipping ahead, always ahead. The men softly whistling. Delicate trills for a raven's ear.

Ray swung back and forth and watched. How nice it would be to stay here in this park. It was beautiful. A good place. But it wasn't home. There were no friends here. No Rogers to sit and visit with. Ray pushed with his feet, giving the swing greater flight. Once back home some kids dared him to do a loop. Swing so hard that he would sail up and over the crossbar. No one had ever done a complete circle loop on the park swings. He could do it if he tried, the kids had told him. Mrs. Rogers warned, "You'll kill yourself doing that crazy swing stuff, if you want to kill yourself join the army. . . ." Ray kicked harder. The air felt good rushing into his open mouth and combing his hair. He leaned back, tucked his legs as the swing curved downward, and then at the low point he jutted them forward, propelling himself higher into the air.

Swooping back and forth, Ray knew something important was happening. His mind was a trellis of thoughts. New images came and went with each thrust of the swing. The brushing of a child's hand against my arm. A birthday song that no one sang. An old lady with a red thread in her blouse. Back and forth.

The taste of a hot dog with mustard. Willie Mays in center field. Ice cream shouldn't melt. They could have told me, they didn't want me.

Mother burned her finger on the birthday candle, it's all right, it's all right, it's not your fault. I got to be the reindeer and lead the parade, all the children played tag with their eyes, hide-and-seek, peekaboo, with me, their friend, they liked me. I didn't mean to get the buttons off, didn't mean to.

Tonalpoulqui said I was an eagle, would fly to the sky, like this, I am. I can see the tops of trees, touch the sun with my feet, see the single red thread in her shawl, see her pretending to be Elvis Presley, see her dead. I tried to keep the map for Butler. I didn't mean to lose it, but I, but I could get another, you want to see, when he comes back. I can find him at the laundromat, across the street, that's where he is, I can tell him the wash is finished and he'll like me again, tell me we are friends, like before. I miss him, wish John Henry were here right now, I could get him a map, if that's what he wants. I promise not to talk no more, won't ask any more questions. I promise.

I can do a loop. Yes, I can. You want to see a loop. I'm not a dummy. Dummy, Dummy. I don't like that. Why call me a dummy, that hurts me, calling me a dummy. My mother doesn't like it, she's dead. She said my friends were coming, they were just late, to put the hats on the table. She said they were just late but I watched and watched and nobody came. Nobody came to my birthday party, they said they would. They called me dummy dummy. I'm not a dummy, I can do a loop, nobody can do a loop. Ray roared higher.

There were other images and ideas just outside his reach. Ray knew they were there. He had seen them before. Now they were here. Waiting for his touch. Prejudice. Friendship. Hostility. Freedom. Intimacy. Life with a woman, a child. Trust. Love. All waited to be held and tested. Hatred. Anger. Generosity. Kindness. All waited to connect with the happenings in Ray's life and make them no longer random. Ray's gaze crisscrossed the sky, afraid and elated. Glad to be alive. Afraid of life. Willing to be an eagle and a man.

The swing reached the peak of its arc—it hung for a second, tempting gravity, then jerked violently earthward. Ray hung on for dear life. The metal poles supporting the swing lifted off the ground as Ray's momentum dragged them upward. Ray feared it was all going to topple over. Then the legs settled back, and Ray squeezed the chains so his swing could slow down. Soon he settled into a gentle curve. There was no longer any impulse to do a loop. Ray coasted awhile. Then dragged his feet to stop the swing. Took a deep breath. And looked at the cobalt sky and the bar that crossed it.

Ray began to cry. It was a cry unlike any he had ever known before. Physical pain was not making him cry. And it was not for joy, either—like when he was with Butler in the pickup truck. He was not crying for what he was missing but for what he understood for the first time. Crying at the wonder of being alive. And liking himself. Crying from the heart. It was as if his soul suddenly took flight. It was an awkward flight, like his tears. Tears stumbled from his eyes, held back, then sobbed loose. Freed. Flooding his mind with gladness. And confusion.

Through this veil of fear and celebration Ray felt someone approach the swing. He remembered that feeling—that night in Golden Gate Park, when he wore the reindeer costume and couldn't see. He could still hear the sound of the swing and the sound of the men coming. Ray gripped the chains, pinched his eyes shut, and tucked his head into his chest. Ray felt his body tremble. Someone stood in front of him. Stood over him. Spoke to him. Ray couldn't make out what the person said. Then he realized the words were English. He prayed that the voice would speak again and also go away.

He heard the slow clank of the swing. Maybe it was the swing that made this noise or a truck or his own fearful imagination. When he heard the voice for a second time, Ray thought it was God speaking. God speaking to him. Yet he didn't know what God meant. The voice repeated itself for the third time. Ray whispered the words to himself. "I am a dentist," and thought out loud—"God is a dentist?"

The person standing in front of Ray laughed. "I am Navarro Alejaudie Jldefonso, a dentist—what can I do for you?" Ray shrugged. He wasn't sure what to do. To trust this stranger and speak with him or to run. Ray tried to run, but his feet didn't respond to his intention. He sat in the swing, petrified by indecision and fear and confusion. The dentist continued to speak.

"My wife and I, and our children, we are here every Sunday, and I looked at you and I seemed to think you were crying, are you well?"

Ray enjoyed listening to the dentist. It was nice to hear his friendliness and concern. It had been so long since anyone had spoken to him that way. He wanted desperately to speak back. Ray peeked at the dentist. He was short and balding and wore wire-frame glasses that seemed to want to fall from his face. The man caught the attention of a woman sitting on a bench not far away. His shoulders hunched, and he threw both hands palm up in an "I don't know" gesture. The woman beckoned for him to return to the bench. But the dentist wasn't ready yet; he shook his head. Then, in a soft voice, he asked Ray, "Are you lost?"

Ray shook his head fervently no. It was easier to be alone. He wanted to be left alone. To solve his own problems. Return to his home.

The dentist persisted. "What are you doing here?" The question frightened Ray. Perhaps this man was a policeman. Would he take him to that jail? Ray began to perspire. He felt his hands slip against the links of the chain. And his heart drummed out of control. The last time Ray tried to talk to anyone on the swing in the park, they kicked him and tried to take the buttons.

The dentist turned and spoke loud enough for both the woman on the bench and Ray to hear. "Do you know the National Park is right here? Do you like to go with us to visit the park?" The woman on the bench shook her head no. The dentist waited for Ray's answer. When Ray couldn't speak, the dentist, in resignation, asked a final "Do you like to go with us to visit the park? Do you have a name?"

Ray's mind raced back and forth. He saw Butler in the truck, and he saw Tonalpoulqui. The men in the park kicking him. He wanted to talk to this stranger, but he just couldn't. It would be better to stay silent. His head turned side to side. The cold solder of fear was closing his mind, binding his heart into stillness. Ray held onto the chains of the swing. Unwilling to let go. He saw the disappointment in the dentist's eyes. Saw the dentist slowly turn and walk away.

Astonishing both himself and the dentist, Ray shouted in a shrill voice, "My name is Raymond Martinez and I live in San Francisco!"

The dentist froze. Then turned toward Ray, a soft smile on his face. His eyes dancing, he put his hands together as if in prayer and responded. "I know, I had this vision. Looking at you on the swing I saw Jesus, the face of Jesus crying."

J. B. Carver, Defender Of The Shadow People

Sherry Croce raced up the stairs and swung open the door to J. B. Carver's office. She was so out of breath she almost stumbled. Carver gawked. He had never seen Miss Croce in such disarray. She was always so prim and—

Sherry yelled, "We've got him!"

"What?" Carver winced.

"Ray Martinez! He's been found in some small town, living with a dentist. The Mexican consulate called. Yahoo!"

"Yahoo," Carver repeated with a controlled and comical tone.

"Yes," Croce yelped. "We've got him, thank god, isn't it wonderful?"

"Wonderful," Carver agreed.

Croce was somewhat taken aback by his lack of enthusiasm. What am I doing wrong, she asked herself. I mean, she expected him . . . to go out and buy her a bottle of champagne. As she gazed around the room, she realized something unusual—and bad—was happening. She asked, "Wh—what is going on here, this place is usually a mess but not this—"

Carver tried to deflect her. "Isn't it time I straightened up a bit?"

Sherry wouldn't have any of it. She walked around Carver's small office, tapping her toe at cartons and packing crates. "What's this here, have they asked you to move or something? I know it isn't your idea to clean this place—did you get transferred?"

Carver thumbed through a pile of papers and then stuffed them into a box. "You know, yesterday, these are my files, my life, and—"

"What's going on?"

Carver finished calmly. "These files are mine, they didn't belong to anyone in Alabama or D.C., they are mine. And yesterday some Bekin brain comes in here, without my permission, and you know they took three of my file cabinets, I don't know where they are, in the basement, over at Bekins, or in some furniture supply office being sold as surplus. Shit! They had no right!"

"Where are you? What's going on here? Why didn't?" Croce shot questions faster than Carver could answer. Conversation crossed . . . mixed . . . missed fire.

"So I'm doing my own house cleaning taking everything home with me. You know." Carver put his hands on one file folder— "They took my papers on the Martinez case, all except for these, they were in my briefcase."

Croce was back thinking about Martinez. "But he's safe. It's all over. We've got him!"

Carver grinned. "Dear lady, this case is not over, where are my files? Who took them? And your Martinez . . . well, the public guardian doesn't want him. Fleming our defender of law and order he's, I think he's pulling a fast one, there's more to this—"

Croce wouldn't let him swamp her confidence and enthusiasm. "I won't hear it, we've got Ray and soon he'll be safe, back in our care. It's you I'm worried about." Croce looked at the frazzled Carver. "I mean you usually look a bit upside down, but look at this place—you want some help?"

Carver knew it was time. "Yeah, I can use a hand."

Carver astonished her. He had never before asked her for help. It worried her. "Is this the J. B. Carver I know?" she asked. "Master detective, defender of the shadow people, hope of the secretarial pool . . ."

J. B. Carver set his eyes on her. It was time to tell her. "This is J. B. Carver, J. B. Carver about to, about to lose his job—three weeks—"

"What!" Sherry cried.

"Three weeks," Carver continued with some re-
newed strength in his voice. "Three weeks, that's what
they gave me. Three weeks—and they stole my files!"

Carver had calmed. He felt relief to finally tell
Sherry that his days on this case and all the other cases
they'd shared were ended. These cases—this was the
bond that held them together. It was the twinning that
kept them going.

Carver handed the file folder to Sherry. "Keep this.
It's my correspondence with the FBI, the lawyers, State
Department, and HEW. Sometimes these lawyers are
connected, and I've caught Mrs. Burr's lawyer, Mr.
Fleming, with his hand in the cookie jar, grabbin' for
crumbs. Maybe it's more. I don't know. Keep this paper
safe."

Now the painful step was over with. Carver
loosened up: "How did you get the word about Ray, who
turned the trick?"

Sherry beamed. "I did, all my own, you know how
the U.S. consulate was telling us nothing. So I got a
hunch and called the Mexican Consular Service; and it's
kinda amazing, but the day I called they also got this call
from a dentist—we both called, I wrote it down here—"
Sherry pulled her note pad from her purse.

Before she could read her notes, Carver was congratulating her. "Nice going, good touch, you want a
job."

"Yes, it's here." She turned pages, smiling. "Doctor
Navarro picked up Raymond Martinez at a park near the
town of Uruapan, Michoacán, Mexico, and gave him
shelter. Then he called the U.S. office in Guadalajara and
they told him they couldn't help so he called the Mexican consulate. Our calls on behalf of Raymond Martinez
were almost simultaneous. You never told me about
luck." Sherry glanced at J. B. Carver. "Dr. Navarro lives
four hours' drive out of Guadalajara."

"So now what?" Carver asked.

"I don't know. I guess we transport Raymond
home."

"I think what we've got to work on . . ." Carver said,

then paused. "He's going to get home all right—we've got to make sure all the paper work is done on this side—can you make sure he's—"

"I thought you were retiring," Sherry said.

"After the case." Carver grinned. "So get his eligibility for ATD straightened out and some subpayee funds approved. We don't want to lose Ray to some institution because his paper work is screwed up. I'm going to work on these lawyers and see if I can get Ray's legal guardianship out of Wilkins' hands and into the P.G. office."

Sherry jotted down a few notes. Then she turned and almost skipped out of Carver's office.

"Nice going kid," Carver called after her.

Carver was right about most things. But he was wrong about how easy it would be to bring Raymond back to the United States. First the U.S. State Department became involved in planning Ray's return. They generated all sorts of detailed and complex plans—bus trips, plane trips, travel aides, manifests, directions, memos, contradictions in triplicate. Then the Mexican government decided it would be easier if they simply expedited the matter. They arranged a bus trip for Raymond from Guadalajara to Mexico City that was to be followed by an airplane flight from Mexico City directly to San Francisco.

But then, on the bus trip between Guadalajara and Mexico City, the bus broke down. Consequently, instead of arriving in Mexico City at six in the evening, it arrived at eight-thirty. By that time, the official who was to meet Raymond upon his arrival and take him to the airport had gone home. Raymond thus found himself alone in one of the largest cities in the world.

Later, the Mexican government cabled San Francisco:

RAYMOND MARTINEZ CANNOT BE LOCATED. HE
IS BELIEVED TO BE IN MEXICO CITY.

Everything Was The Same Yet Somehow Different

July 10, 1972

The city that Raymond Martinez found himself in was populated by five million citizens, all of whom seemed to stream about this lost pilgrim. Unaware of his intent stare. Perhaps momentarily conscious of his country clothes and his new shoes. The shoes hurt. Raymond considered standing at the bus depot and waiting. Someone would come. Then he started walking. It was early evening, and many were out enjoying the cool night air: shopping, going to a movie, or simply strolling in the parks and wide streets. Ray joined the flow. When the flow slowed or trickled, he sought out more populated streets.

He walked down the Avenue of Juarez past the National Palace, La Professor, and House of Tiles. The buildings along the way were lighted with great arc lamps and trimmed with colored bulbs. Ray thought of his room at Mrs. Burr's. He, too, had colored lamps. Only they didn't work. And the Alameda Central. A park of quivering trees.

The crowd flowed and turned down the grand Paseo de la Reforma. Ray followed. He passed the National Lottery Building, with its blinking lights and colorful placards. And took pleasure in the brightly decorated magazine racks. The lingering. The vapor trail behind a car's tail lamp. Men in T-shirts leaning with one leg propped against the buildings. Women in threes: child, mother, grandmother. Three generations walking together. Holding hands. He enjoyed the smells of food cooking. Fruit squeezed into juices or cut into edible chunks. Enjoyed seeing the people sitting on benches while children circled around them in their play. It was like his park. The park by the merry-go-round. Then—without warning—Raymond was home.

It was a big building with an iron gate. Not lighted like the others. But it was his home. He *knew*. He was certain. A small bronze plaque was attached to the iron gate. It was the American Embassy. Ray curled up beneath the gate and drifted toward sleep.

Before slipping into unconsciousness, Ray called to mind one more time the things that mattered to him. He hummed "Love Me Tender," then "Amazing Grace." He thought of Tonalpoulqui. Saw the chickens in the back of the pickup. Remembered driving the truck with one hand, like Butler. The taste of *pulque*—he could still feel its sting. Talking rocks. Tonalpoulqui's eyes closed to earthly vision. Willie Mays, Elvis Presley, Star Flower, John Henry Butler—his galaxy of gods. He repeated the chants for rain and praised the eagle. Ray gazed upward at the plaque on the gate. The plaque had the engraving of a great eagle. Tonalpoulqui had told him that his home was with eagles. Everything had its place. He put his hand into his pocket and clutched his reflector button. His breath escaped into the night air, forming faint clouds as he spoke to himself. "Willie Mays' last home run in a San Francisco uniform, he hit number six hundred and forty-six at Cincinnati." Ray Martinez was home.

Chocolate Candy Sticks To Your Hands

J. B. Carver found out about Ray's guardianship hearing only by chance. He was saying his good-byes in the D.A.'s office when a secretary tipped him that the hearing was going to begin in just a few minutes. Seems the public guardian's office wanted to let this case slip by, didn't want to assume legal responsibility for Ray. So when Wilkins initiated a hearing to place Ray back in the care of Mrs. Burr, the office chose simply not to oppose his intention.

Carver telephoned Sherry to meet him right away, then raced to the city hall courtroom where Ray's future was being decided.

In the courtroom, a probate commissioner presided at a large central table. His name was Frank DiGrigoli; he was known to favor placement in board-and-care homes rather than state institutions. DiGrigoli's face was ghostly gray and sagged to the left. A stroke had left him partially paralyzed. He sat leaning to one side, and with his good hand he kept adjusting his robe so it wouldn't fall from his left shoulder.

Wilkins, the lawyer, sat across the table from Di-Grigoli. He was neatly dressed in a tiger-striped suit, lawyer's vest, and thin tie. Behind Wilkins, in the first row of chairs, sat Mrs. Burr, eating from a box of chocolates. Sitting next to her—there he was—Raymond Martinez. This was the first time Carver had actually encountered Ray; and now, to his great surprise, the man did not look at all like what he expected. Ray didn't look weird, dim, or strange—except maybe that the baseball cap was a little unexpected. The man next to Mrs. Burr was good-looking—in fact, he looked like a skinny Elvis Presley. He was dressed in new clothes with his hair slicked back under the well-worn orange and black cap. When he recognized Ray, Carver wanted to rush up and introduce himself, but decorum wouldn't allow that; and Fleming was in the process of finishing up his opening remarks to the commissioner.

"So it's my contention that a reasonable guardian, someone who is familiar with Mr. Martinez, someone who is a responsible citizen—not an impersonal governmental agency—should assume legal guardianship of my client." As Wilkins was speaking. Carver moved down to the table where two commissioners sat, making sure no one was unaware of his entrance. Behind him, Sherry entered the room and quietly took an aisle seat several rows away from the commissioners' table.

"Well," Wilkins said, looking pointedly at Carver, "I'm glad, Commissioner, that finally someone from the public guardian's office has shown up. I've tried through every legal and off-the-record way to get the public guardian's office to assume . . ."

"I'm not here from them," Carver interrupted. "I don't represent the public guardian's office."

"Then who?" Wilkins snapped.

"Who, sir, do you represent? Are you employed by this city or have an interest in this case?" the commissioner asked with a slight stammer. He punctuated his question by lifting a lifeless left arm from his lap with his right hand and placing the dead arm on the table.

"My name is James Carver," he said. "I supervise the fraud investigation unit of DPSS and with Miss Croce, the social worker in this case"—he indicated who she was—"I think we have important information related to this hearing."

The commissioner tapped his pencil in Sherry's direction and asked with a cough, "Umm, Miss Croce, uh huh, do you represent your office in this matter?"

"Yes!" she said, rising nervously to her feet. The commissioner reminded her of her father—a body half paralyzed by stroke.

"Sit down, girl, you look worried," the commissioner said, not unkindly. "It's all right, we're here to find out the facts in this case."

. Fleming moved to the end of the table as far away from Carver as possible. Drawing his briefcase toward him, he outlined the case as he saw it. "As I said before this interruption, I filed—you have the papers—for a removal of guardianship. And in a June ninth hearing—I think you have that in front of you as well—the guardian's office refused to take this case. It says right there in the court record that they recommend—as I am suggesting today—that a private citizen assume this responsibility."

The commissioner shook his head in weary agreement, relieved that the hearing would soon be over. He would hear who this lawyer recommended; then he would grant guardianship to whoever that was. It was an act he performed six times a day, four days a week.

Wilkins continued. "In accordance with this recommendation, I have asked Mrs. Burr, who at one time was the board-and-care operator for Raymond Martinez, to assume, with your approval, ummm, this position. There is no one else." Wilkins swept around in a dramatic survey of the nearly vacant courtroom. "There is no one else, as you can see. . . . Mr. Martinez has only one living relative, an aunt who is quite elderly and in need of physical care. We are very fortunate in this case that Mrs. Burr has agreed to take on the responsibility of guardianship."

Mrs. Burr sat up at the mention of her name and put her hand in the air as if she were about to take an oath.

The commissioner motioned with a wave of his own hand that Mrs. Burr need not rise.

"Sir," Carver barked, angry and fearful that things might be nearly out of his control. "Sir, I have information, I honestly, it would be a miscarriage—Mrs. Burr there is not a reliable, I have information that she is criminally involved—" Carver began a frantic search for his notes.

"Frankly," Wilkins shouted, jabbing his finger toward Carver, "this problem is all the responsibility of the social services office—they should have placed Mr. Martinez in the care of the public guardian's office upon the receipt of his estate!" Wilkins' confidence had carried him too far.

"Has Mr. Martinez received an estate?" the commissioner asked.

"Yes," Sherry yelped, and then shyly rose to her feet. "Ray Martinez has inherited over twenty thousand dollars!"

"Thank you." The commissioner waggled his head.

"That's my point," Wilkins charged. "If the department hadn't neglected its responsibility, then I wouldn't have become involved, I've really—"

"Who's the guardian now?" asked the commissioner.

"Henry Butler!" Carver reported, still digging into his pockets. Mrs. Burr shifted ponderously to one side so she could see the commissioner. Carver continued. "John Henry Butler, who is Mrs. Burr's stepson, is under warrant in three states for forgery, and I think it can be proved he abducted Ray Martinez and abandoned him in Mexico with the full knowledge of Mrs. Burr here and their lawyer, Mr. Wilkins. They all planned together to steal Ray's inheritance—"

"Your honor," Wilkins roared, slamming his briefcase closed. "I mean commissioner, this is absurd! I am being, it's being implied here that I am guilty of complicity in this matter; that I somehow arranged these . . ."

The commissioner's pencil drummed nervously against the desk. "Mr. Wilkins," he said after a few moments, "what is your relationship to the guardian Mr. Butler?"

"Commissioner, this case came to me from the lawyer's panel," Fleming said, regaining his composure. "I did not seek it out nor have I benefited in any unusual way. In fact, I have worked without remuneration on behalf of Mrs. Burr, Mr. Butler, and most of all, Mr. Martinez."

The room was silent as Wilkins piled argument on top of argument, his hands working like a bricklayer. "Mr. Butler's illicit activity came to my attention in April of this year and again *I* was the one who had to alert the department of social services, *I* was the one who had to file for a change in guardianship, and now *I* am again trying to get Raymond into a safe home. I think Mrs. Burr can and will provide personal care as Raymond's legal guardian." Wilkins felt the scale of opinion tilting in his favor. He carefully set the briefcase upright.

Carver tried a long shot. He took his wallet from his coat pocket and removed a crumpled piece of paper from the billfold compartment. Slowly, he unfolded the document. The paper was an old laundry list. Quietly and deliberately, Carver pretended to read. "I have here an inventory of money received by Mrs. Burr—inherited money that belonged to Ray Martinez. This money—" Carver looked up from the list and directly at Mrs. Burr. "This money was received by Mrs. Burr as early as January of this year."

Wilkins blanched. He had moved around the corner of the table and was now on the same side as the commissioner. He summoned all his legal presence and began an argument that seemed well rehearsed. "Yes, Mrs. Burr received some money on behalf of Ray Martinez." Placing both hands flat on the table, he leaned forward and continued. "Mrs. Burr believed that she was the legal guardian of Ray Martinez, since at that time she was providing *total* care for Mr. Martinez through her board-and-care license. So she accepted the money for Ray—"

"Did she accept the money," Carver broke in, "claiming to be the legal guardian? Isn't that the moment when she approached you to ask you to arrange for her or her son to become Ray's legal guardian?"

"Please let me conduct this hearing," the commissioner cautioned.

Wilkins ground the palms of his hands into the top of the table as though he were stubbing out a cigarette. "I advised Mrs. Burr to deposit the money in a bank account for Raymond, which she did." Wilkins' voice seemed faint.

"When did she set up this account? Was it a trust account?" Carver pressed. "How much is left in that account now?"

Wilkins turned to the commissioner. "Do I have to answer these questions?" His hands, which had danced with each eloquent argument, now appeared pinned to the table. "This all seems unrelated to the purpose of this hearing, and Mr. Carver has no official—"

"Go ahead, answer," came a sharp reply from the commissioner.

Wilkins stood up straight and took a labored breath. "Well, let's see," he struggled. "The account was set up, um, several weeks ago."

Carver had him. Sherry Croce almost clapped, then clenched her hands together. Carver was shaking. DiGrigoli turned toward Mrs. Burr. His gaze was withering. "This sounds like a case of misrepresentation by you, Mrs. Burr, legally accepting money when you were not the guardian and disguising the fact from this court. I want a full accounting of that money, something I'm sure your lawyer will help you with. As for you, Mr. Wilkins, as the attorney for this arrangement, I find your involvement less than commendable." The commissioner pushed back his robe. "Is Mr. Martinez in the room?"

"Yes," replied Wilkins.

"I would like to speak with Mr. Martinez before making my decision on this matter. Mr. Martinez—"

Ray stood up and answered, "Yes."

"Do you understand, Mr. Martinez, that your attorney, Mr. Wilkins, is arguing that your welfare is best served by placing you in the custody of Mrs. Burr—do you know Mrs. Burr?"

"Yes," Ray answered.

"It is this court's duty to determine whether your affairs should be assigned to the public guardian's office, which means they will handle your money and allow you to stay in the board-and-care home in which you currently reside. Is that clear?"

"Yes," Ray nodded.

"Or I can assign Mrs. Burr here to be your legal guardian, as your attorney requests, and you can return to live at her residence."

"Mrs. Burr has a new facility," Mr. Wilkins interjected, "licensed by the city of San Francisco, and welcomes Mr. Martinez into—"

"Be quiet!" the commissioner rasped. "I want to ask Mr. Martinez some questions. Mr. Martinez, how much money do you have?"

Ray pushed his hand into his pocket and pulled out a new wallet. Unfolding the wallet, Ray fumbled with the zipper. After several attempts, he unzipped an inside compartment and displayed several dollar bills. Ray began to explain. "This is a secret place for money. That's why I—"

Wilkins interrupted. "Commissioner, I have clear psychiatric evidence that Raymond Martinez is not capable of handling or understanding—"

"I think it's clear from the evidence here that you have not, Mr. Wilkins, responsibly handled his financial matters. I suggest you remain silent!"

"Ask Ray if he can add this typical gas and electric bill for the Burr residence!" Wilkins snapped, unwilling to give in.

"That's unfair!" Sherry shouted. "Ray's never *seen* a P G & E bill. And that's the point. At Mrs. Burr's he doesn't get to work on independent living skills. There's not even a phone for him. The one phone is downstairs, and he's not even allowed—"

"Stop, stop!" The commissioner slapped his hand on the desk. "You are all way in front of me. It's Mr. Martinez that I'm interested in hearing from." Having achieved a temporary calm, the commissioner pointed to Ray and asked, "What are you planning to do with that money of yours?"

Ray grinned. "Buy a guitar so I can sing for people."

Wilkins slumped in his chair. "See, your honor, what I was saying, a guitar?"

The commissioner paid no attention to Wilkins' dramatics. "Are you a good singer?" he asked Ray.

"Yes."

"How much money do you have there in your hand?"

"A lot—look." Ray showed everyone in the room that he had three dollars.

"I want you to do me a favor," the commissioner asked. "You will do me a favor, won't you?"

"Yes."

"I want you, I want you, Mr. Martinez, to give your money to *one* person in this room."

"All of it?" Ray asked.

"Yes," the commissioner replied.

Ray took the money in hand and walked toward Mr. Wilkins. Mr. Wilkins smiled and put out his hand, but Ray walked past and seemed confused. Ray hovered in the front of the hearing room, walking first toward Miss Croce and then toward the impassive Mrs. Burr.

"Have you decided?" asked the commissioner.

Mrs. Burr slowly stood up. It was a labored effort that drew Ray's attention. Mrs. Burr was skilled in these matters. She knew Ray. His kind. His needs. His craving for attention. And she knew these hearings. The players. Their flaws. Mrs. Burr put down her chocolates and straightened her dress. Then swelled to her full size. "Lawyers, social workers, you're all the same," she announced. "You talk about cases like numbers. You like this, don't you, this game you play? Now it's my turn. Let me ask you *one* question.

"You, Miss Croce, always suspicious, always inspecting, always hitting my sofa to see if it's dusty or peeking into the refrigerator to check my food. Will *you* take Ray Martinez to live with *you*? I don't hear you asking to have him eat meals with you, now do I? Do *you* want Raymond yammering in your ear all day? Well, will you take him into your home?"

Sherry sat wordless and pale.

"You, Mr. what's your name, Mr. Carver, how about you? When is the last time you had to deal with a kid you couldn't control or had to tie a grown-up man to his bed because he kept falling out all night or kept wandering into the street for who knows what reason? Do you want this Raymond you care so much about, know so much about? Do you want him living with you, lighting fires in the bathroom?" Carver folded the paper in his hands and tucked it into a pocket.

"I thought as much," Mrs. Burr pronounced and spindled one finger into the desk. "I'm the only one here that really wants him, isn't that so?"

Even the commissioner seemed numbed by Mrs. Burr's statement. He knew, like everyone else in the room, that she was telling a perverse truth. That in the end she was the only one waiting for Ray.

Only one person there did not agree with her. He stood in the front of the room with three dollars held above his head. He had come to his own conclusions about what should be done with him. Ray Martinez started to leave the courtroom. He walked past the city and county calendar and the golden bear flag, then straight for the mahogany doors.

"Wait!" the commissioner ordered. "Where are you going?"

Ray spun around and faced the startled faces of the people who were trying to control his life. There was Mrs. Burr, smirking as she always did when she wanted something. And Wilkins, "his" lawyer, was sweating. Sherry Croce smiled and held her hands out as though she were about to hug a child. The commissioner, behind the table, seemed to be in pain; his hand was rubbing his chest. And the big black man—what's his name?—he was just grinning. Ray thought that the grinning man looked a lot like Willie Mays.

Once again, the commissioner asked, "Well, Mr. Martinez, the decision is yours. Who would you give that money to?"

Ray touched the brim of his cap like a pitcher at the start of his move. Then he carefully held the money at arm's length. "I think—" Ray paused. "I think I'd be the best person to keep this money. I'll keep it myself."

There was a long, stunned silence. Until the commissioner broke into gales of laughter. A few moments later, still chuckling, he spoke. "Mr. Martinez, I personally think that you are right, that you can with some time and help manage your own affairs. And I don't think that help will come from your current attorney or his client Mrs. Burr. Therefore, I'm going to commend your case to the public guardian's office, requesting that they administer any inheritance past or future and find you a suitable board-and-care environment that is agreeable both to you and to your social worker, Miss Croce. Is this clear to everyone in this hearing? Then I consider this case closed."

Ray approached the commissioner. "Do you want," he asked, "would you like me to sing a song? I can sing good."

The commissioner was stuffing papers into his brief-case. He hesitated, then smiled. His robe slid off his shoulder. "Yes"—he nodded—"I'd like to hear you. What is it that you sing?"

"Do you like Elvis?"

"Love him."

Epilogue

The Ray who returned to San Francisco was simply not the same person who had been "abandoned" by the care givers assigned to him, classified "incompetent" by the state of California, and decreed by his church to be "without reason." He could speak and read some Spanish and could clearly describe in English his intention to live a normal life. He was no longer dependent on others for his everyday needs. On his own, in a strange place, he had learned to survive and take care of himself.

Although his finances were placed under the super-vision of the public guardian's office and he was assigned a board-and-care home, Ray decided to support himself and to live with people of his own choosing. Ray's first job was at McDonald's on the corner of Haight and Stan-yan. He washed windows, swept the street, and provided food service. This McDonald's faces the entrance to Golden Gate Park and Ray's favorite place—Children's Playground.

Today Ray is happily married to Sandy Cruz Martinez, and they live in San Francisco with Sandy's grandmother. In 1980, Ray and Sandy had a son—Raymond Martinez, Junior. Ray Junior is a completely normal child. Or as Sandy puts it, "He climbs all over the place and won't put his toys away, and he likes to swing on the swing a lot. And he likes people, like his father. And you know he's going to start school next year, *real* school, isn't that nice?"

Although Raymond and his family are eligible for full disability payments, Ray holds down both a full-time and a part-time job. He wants to make ends meet on his own. And yet Ray's ability to live an independent life is still held on a string by the public guardian's office of San Francisco. As legal guardians, they determine the money Ray's family receives from a variety of government agencies. All of which is deducted from Ray's full- and part-time salaries.

In 1982, the guardian's office erroneously allowed these agencies to overpay the Martinez family. When Sandy's grandmother, Sandy, and Ray, along with their social worker, pointed out that their monthly checks were too large, the guardian's office told them not to worry. This was a common problem. Our error would be corrected in due course.

But when the public guardian's office and the various other government agencies involved looked into the matter, they concluded that Ray himself was the problem. His ability to earn his own income screwed up the system. Their solution was to ask Ray to turn over his paychecks directly to the public guardian's office, which would then provide him with an "allowance." The remainder would be used to repay the agencies.

Ray refuses to cooperate with them in this. "This is nothing new," says Ray's social worker. "It's a constant battle of regulation changes, waivers, faulty payments, closing programs, deductions, reviews—we have to get Ray's conservatorship changed so that he can be his own legal guardian and control his own life." But for Ray it's a much simpler matter. "I won't give up my paychecks," he says. "I won't wait in lines. No more."

As for the twenty-thousand-dollar inheritance that should have gone to Ray, well, all of it is gone. He received maybe two thousand dollars of it, paid to him in lieu of his monthly social security benefits. The remainder was siphoned off by John Henry Butler, Mrs.

Burr, and their lawyers. Butler himself remains a fugitive. His stepmother, Mrs. Burr, continues to operate board-and-care homes in San Francisco. She currently oversees two facilities and plans to open a third.

Sherry Croce and J. B. Carver are no longer social workers. Mr. Carver is currently working for the city of Chicago as a youth counselor. Miss Croce retired from the San Francisco Department of Social Services and lives alone in the Sunset District of San Francisco.

Remember Jake, the police horse? Well, he also retired from service. Jake is running around on a pasture someplace in Napa County. Upon Jake's retirement, the city of San Francisco gave a party and unveiled a bronze plaque to honor his faithful service to the citizens of San Francisco and their children. The tribute is located at the Polo Fields stable.

I remember from my own childhood the playground in Golden Gate Park. I remember the carousel and those strange people with the glow knit caps. They always sat facing the carousel on the same benches. I must have wandered close to their bench one day, because I remember one man wanted to give me his sandwich. I was interested in the orange cap. So he gave me that. My mother never did guess where that hat came from. Or maybe she knew all along.

Today I take my own daughter there. Friends with glow knit caps are still sitting on their bench. Giving up their lunch for the asking. Tipping their hands to say hello. And if we are lucky and it's a sunny day, I can point to the swings and tell my daughter, "See that man over there, the man sitting on the swing with a child in his lap? That man is a very good friend of mine. He's a man called Ray."

ABOUT THE AUTHOR

RON JONES has been a teacher for over 20 years, often in unusual, difficult and controversial positions that have since become the inspiration for his writing. His early experiences as a counselor at a summer camp for handicapped children were reflected in THE ACORN PEOPLE, which was made into an award-winning TV movie. Another TV movie, THE WAVE, was based on a story in his collection, NO SUBSTITUTE FOR MADNESS, about his experiments with his history class at Cubberley High School in Palo Alto. A later teaching job, in the psychiatric ward of a large city hospital, became the basis for KIDS CALLED CRAZY.

In 1972, Jones founded the Zephyros Educational Exchange, a non-profit group of parents, artists and teachers that write, print and distribute their own teaching materials. He has also self-published all his own books previous to SAY RAY. Since 1978 he has been physical education director at San Francisco's Recreation Center of the Handicapped, where he works with 1,200 physically and mentally disabled children and adults, and where he met the real Ray Martinez. He lives with his wife Deanna, a professional potter, and daughter Hilary in the Haight-Ashbury section of San Francisco.

We Deliver!
And So Do These Bestsellers.

SPECIAL
MONEY SAVING
OFFER

Now you can have an up-to-date listing of Bantam's hundreds of titles plus take advantage of our unique and exciting bonus book offer. A special offer which gives you the opportunity to purchase a Bantam book for only 50¢. Here's how!

By ordering any five books at the regular price per order, you can also choose any other single book listed (up to a $4.95 value) for just 50¢. Some restrictions do apply, but for further details why not send for Bantam's listing of titles today!

Just send us your name and address plus 50¢ to defray the postage and handling costs.

DON'T MISS
THESE CURRENT
Bantam Bestsellers